SEDUCTIVE SILENCE

A STEAMY STUTTER ROMANCE

LARISSA LYONS

This series is dedicated to anyone who has difficulty speaking up for themselves. May you find a way to be heard.

And for my dear Mr. Lyons who's always requesting another Regency; here you go, you spectacular man. (Sorry I don't enjoy housework and cleaning the kitchen as much as I do escaping to 1815.)

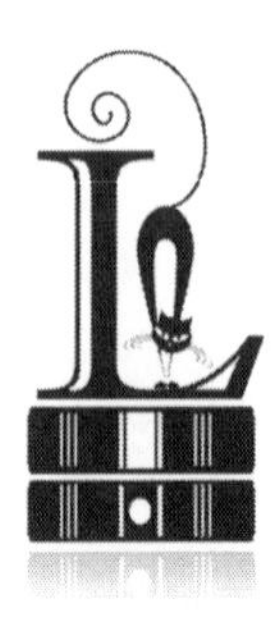

Published by Literary Madness

ISBN 978-1-949426-10-6 Paperback (August 2021 Rev.)
ISBN 978-1-949426-08-3 E-book (May 2021 Rev.)

Proofread by Judy Zweifel at Judy's Proofreading; Copy edits by ELF at elewkfl@yahoo.com; Edited by Elizabeth St. John

At Literary Madness, we strive to create a book free of typos. If you notice anything amiss, we're happy to fix it. litmadness@yahoo.com

CONTENTS

SEDUCTIVE SILENCE

1. The Mistress Conundrum 9
2. To Be or Not to Be...A Fallen Woman 39
3. To Converse Over Dinner – Or Not 62
4. Bird-Witted as a Cuckoo or Lucky as a Lark? 88
5. Past vs Present vs Passion 110
6. Tawdry or Titillating? 'Tis a Matter of Opinion... 140

Lusty Letters Excerpt 171
A FREE story - The Pirate's Pleasure 181
About Larissa 183
More Bang-up Regencies 185
Larissa's Booklist 191

SEDUCTIVE SILENCE

He listened in perfect silence. She wished him to speak, but he would not.

— JANE AUSTEN, *EMMA*

1

THE MISTRESS CONUNDRUM

My mistress' eyes are nothing like the sun;
If hairs be wires, black wires grow on her head.
I have seen roses damask, red and white,
But no such roses see I in her cheeks;
And in some perfumes is there more delight
Than in the breath that from my mistress reeks.

William Shakespeare, "Sonnet CXXX"

London, 1815

"'Than in the b-breath that from my mistress reeks.'" Daniel Holbrook, the fourth Marquis of Tremayne, repeated the last few words with a grim smile.

"Reeks is right," he muttered beneath his breath

(breath that most assuredly did *not* reek of onions as that of his former mistress often had). He crumpled the topmost page off the stack he'd liberated from a desk drawer and tossed it over his shoulder.

When it bounced against the window coverings and crinkled to the floor, a curious sort of satisfaction threatened to dissipate his gloom. With great zeal, he balled up more of the filled pages that had been languishing in his desk ever since her ill-fated demand.

Poems. Stupid poems.

Said *former* mistress had begged him to memorize and recite poetic verse to her. Though he'd—wisely—refrained from succumbing to her urging, Shakespeare's 130 had been the only sonnet to remotely tempt him into performing.

Thinking of her likely response to his stumbling recital, assuming she perceived the intended slight and took affront, a real laugh emerged. Cy huffed a surprised bark at the sound, the first Daniel had heard from his faithful, snoozing companion since the damnable rain had caused man and beast to retreat to the safety of his study. Now, with drapes drawn and fire roaring, he sought to forget the downpour lashing the house and the dark memories apt to drown him.

He'd only taken to cleaning *out* his desk in order to avoid what resided *on* it—an advertisement he'd saved and Penry's unanswered note: *Are you still planning to attend the festivities this eve? Lest you forget, you already agreed.*

Ahhh, the "festivities". Amorous festivities, no doubt.

Was he going to attend?

Daniel didn't rightly know. He fingered his bruised jaw, working it from side to side. The swelling had gone down to the point he didn't think he'd terrify a potential inamorata with his battered visage. But what if he did?

Mayhap 'twould be a good thing—scare off any candidates *before* he opened his mouth.

Was replacing the reeking Louise really something that had to be done tonight?

Just to hear the potentially uplifting crackle, he hefted several bunched-up poetic missiles overhead into the burgundy drapes. Cy gave a curious sniff, his languid gaze following one paper ball when it rolled drunkenly toward him.

Louise. Sometimes he'd thought marbles resided in her upper garret. But he'd tolerated her less-than-desirable qualities in exchange for the ones he did like. Most notably, her mouth.

Fact was, despite her off-putting fondness for onions, he'd often found her mouth worthy of appreciation (if not its very own sonnet), for she typically kept it open and active, chattering about everything yet saying nothing. He could spend two nights a week in her company and only be called upon to utter a handful of sentences per fortnight.

Add her lack of expectation for meaningful conversation to her lusty fervor for lovemaking and was it any wonder he'd made her his mistress a decade ago at the absurd age of twenty-one?

His long nap complete, Cy stretched and sauntered over, placing his ugly mug on the desk until he received the expected scratch behind his ears, then thanking his master with a sloppy bark. Daniel blotted the ever-present drool with the handkerchief he kept at the ready. He'd rescued the one-eyed mangy mongrel, now plump on doggie pudding and old age, when he'd caught the scarecrow of a pup being whipped for making off with the baker's meat pasties. A coin flipped in his direction persuaded the baker to turn over the dog. A meat pasty in Daniel's outstretched hand persuaded the frightened animal to follow.

It might have taken several years and several hundred hours to win the canine's trust, but Daniel had accomplished the deed, and gladly. He had no use for those who beat others, whether they had four legs or two.

Cyclops gave a hearty whine and pushed past Daniel to nuzzle the drapes aside where he promptly pressed his nose to the windowpane, the unrelenting storm on the other side making a hash of the view.

Daniel frowned at the grey sky. *I know, mate. I detest this weather too.*

But he detested more the dance necessary to find a new mistress. Waltzing the pretty and paying glib compliments to secure a warm and willing body in his bed might prove to be his undoing. Of a certainty, contemplating it posed significantly more pain than Penry's lightning jab, else he would have seen the task done before now.

Gad. Ten weeks.

His head clunked forward into his waiting hands. Ten blighted weeks equating to seventy long nights he'd palmed his staff rather than find another ladybird to do the job for him.

He scrubbed at his hair as though the friction would lessen the growing tension centered in his groin. Blast. If he chuffed his pipe any more frequently, he'd likely yank the thing off.

The momentary ease such release brought was just that—a few seconds' respite from urges growing ever more insistent. A surging morning erection growing ever more persistent. "I need a woman."

"Well, aren't you the fortunate one?" A decidedly feminine voice jerked his head upright. "Just as you call out to the universe, I present myself in all my wilted glory."

Raking his hair into some semblance of order, Daniel skewered his sister with a glare. He hated being caught unawares.

Beyond the glass panes Cy had revealed, rain drizzled freely and her fashionable attire did the same. The once pristine walking dress, made of the palest cream French cambric and complete with intricately fringed hem, was topped off with a fur-trimmed spencer in what was supposed to be a coordinating spring green. Wet, it looked more like something Cyclops had cast up after emptying one of Daniel's snuff boxes.

What a decline for the costly toggery (he should know; he'd paid enough for it when she'd spied the plate in *Ackermann's* and pleaded with him to have it made up). Evaluating it now, he doubted the finely woven cambric would ever return to its former, undrizzled-upon glory.

The delicate, coordinating parasol he'd commissioned as a surprise had obviously been a waste of his blunt—it was bound up tight, *unused*. Everything else dripped and sagged. Her once-new bonnet, her dark blond hair beneath. And the spencer's fur trim? "You have a...dead ferret strangling your neck. What b-brings you here this fine spring...day?"

And damn him for remembering so much about ladies' stylish apparel. Useless information, now that he'd seen his precious Elizabeth matched in a happy union.

All smiles and sunshine despite her disastrous, dripping attire, she swept toward him, pointing that conspicuously dry parasol his direction. "Ridicule all you want. It won't do any good. I'm in a lovely state of mind and have no intention of allowing anything to alter it."

She paused to scratch Cy beneath his chin when he bounded toward her. "And aren't you the most remarkable boy?" Her shining eyes found Daniel's. "Sometimes I forget how good he looks. In my mind, he's still the scrawny bag of bones you described in your letters." Elizabeth had only been in town a short while. Married in the country last fall, she'd spent the time since living on her husband's estate and the majority of time before chained to their father's.

When Cy began snuffing at her hand, Elizabeth laughed and returned her attention to the dog. "I do apologize, Sir Cyclops, but I don't have any treats. Ann's in the kitchen"—she mentioned her lady's maid—"I wager she'll sneak you a dollop of whatever's to be had."

"What he needs. Mmm—" Surprised rather than frustrated when his lips unexpectedly stuck together, Daniel faked a cough into his fist, and then finished, "More food."

Ignoring the scowl in his voice, Elizabeth ushered the dog toward the door and asked one of the hovering footmen to escort Cyclops downstairs.

An identical pair, his footmen were, twins he'd picked up years ago when they were but mere lads engaged in pilfering pockets on the dirty streets of London. One named John, the other James. Only James went by "Buttons", a childhood nickname Daniel knew he'd butcher. B's might not be as bad as D's, but they were close, so he'd renamed the boy "*Swift* John" the day they'd met and to this day called him thus.

While Swift John watched with a knowing grin, Elizabeth whispered something to John before relinquishing the dog into his care. Daniel suspected she went to the trouble because her maid was sweet on John rather than any real desire to see the dog off.

Her matchmaking duties done, she whirled round and came in. “Thank you, Buttons,” she said as his remaining footman moved to close the door behind her. Wasting no time, she marched straight to the curtains behind his desk and hauled them open.

The metal rings clacking along the rod sounded like gunfire and Daniel barely masked his wince. But he needn’t have bothered. She was busy gathering up the crushed pages and, after seeing the lyrical lines Louise had penned upon them, tossing the whole lot into the rubbish bin.

“What have you been up to? Providing Cyclops new toys to chase after?” Her tidying efforts complete, she straightened and grinned, her brown gaze fairly shimmering with joy. “Rain or no, it’s too glorious a day to shroud yourself up like this.”

Coming up beside him, she relinquished the frilly parasol and placed it square on his desk—still spring green, he idly noted, and not the muddy color of Cy’s snuff-induced cascade as was the rest of her gown. Next she took off her bonnet, the silk flowers planted among lace and pintucking every bit as wilted and bedraggled as the rest of her. “And I can’t believe you’d waste the fuel on a fire, as muggy as it is outside. Don’t tell me my big brother is turning into an old maid?”

Granted, along with everyone else he’d been enjoying the unusually mild week, but all that changed with the latest deluge that chilled the air, and his soul. Avoiding the topic—something he excelled at—he plucked at the parasol's dangling fringe, as arid as a desert, and gave her sopping dress a speaking glance. "Useful item."

"Stop that." She slapped his hand away and smoothed the fringe. "It's my very favorite, as you well know. I tucked it under my dress so it wouldn't get wet."

"Ah now." Recalling how he'd just mangled the sound, he took a slow breath before continuing. "Makes...total sense. And the reason for your visit?"

He was curious what would bring her out in such weather. Not that he wasn't pleased to see her. The one member of his immediate family who still drew breath. More than that, the one member who'd never betrayed him—either in fact or by dying too damn soon.

With her customary composure, his sister took possession of the leather chair flanking his desk and evaluated him as one might a captured butterfly. Her brows drew into a frown. "Why is half your face a veritable bevy of purple and green?"

"Half?" He barely refrained from fingering his lip. The new scab over the old scar had dropped off two days ago. "Ellie, surely you em...bellish."

"Not by much," she muttered. "Covered in whiskers, it still shines through." She rose and approached him. "I fear 'tis becoming unseemly, Daniel, this fascination you have for sporting rainbows." Elizabeth turned his head with gentle fingers to inspect the worst of it. Lips pursed, she released him to rummage in the reticule dangling from her wrist. "When will you realize you no longer need to prove yourself?"

When I stop hiding in here every time it rains.

Hiding in his study, where his mechanical pursuits provided the solace nature denied him. He glanced over at one apparatus in particular and felt a grimace tighten his cheeks. When they worked, that was.

"Silence. I should have known. Your answer to everything unpleasant."

Daniel glanced back at Elizabeth. His bad memories weren't to be laid at her doorstep. Neither was his sour mood. "If I recite p-p-*po*-etry, will you smile?"

That got a laugh from her. "The day you recite poetry is the day I juggle torches standing on my head."

"Unlit ones, I hope." Relieved he could still smile, he suffered through the application of the lotion she'd pulled from her bag. She was always slathering him with some concoction or other "to help with the bruising and aid healing".

He should be grateful, but the stuff put him in mind of an apothecary. Nose wrinkling by the time she finished, Daniel jerked his head back. "What's in there? Smells like a harem."

Elizabeth stumbled in her efforts to screw the lid on. "A harem? My, where your mind veers..." Jar sealed, she slid it across his desk in between stacks of yet-to-be-crumbled-and-discarded pitiful poetry.

"I tried a different blend this time," she admitted without meeting his gaze.

What else had she chopped and crushed and stirred in there? "Ellie?"

"I think it smells rather lovely."

He sniffed again and frowned. There was more to it than that, over and above the smell. "Out with it."

"Oh, very well." A tiny huff and she finally met his gaze. "If you must know, I added a wee bit of honeysuckle. For hope."

"And?" Although, by now, he was almost past caring. His face felt better than it had since the practice round that landed such a fierce chop to his jaw. He was even starting to like the scent—a little light and fluffy for his tastes to be sure, but it did have a spicy undercurrent, a bit of zest.

"Clovesforlove," she said in one breath.

"Huh?"

"Cloves. To attract love."

"Ellie." His sister and her potions. Romantic whimsy, her and her "spells" for happiness—usually his. But she stood there, looking at him so earnestly, so drippingly—and his face felt so damn comfortable—that all he did was tuck the jar into his newly cleared desk drawer. "Thank you."

Her witchy rescue cream accepted, she resumed her seat and fixed him with one of her sunny smiles. "Surely you can cultivate an interest in something *other* than smashing your face into your friends' fists?"

Daniel's eyes again veered toward the orrery collection occupying the bulk of his study. Nothing gave him greater satisfaction than tinkering with the mechanics of the planetarium models he'd collected. But his satisfaction had dimmed considerably since resurrecting and repairing (or attempting to) the pinnacle of all the models he'd amassed: the one originally owned by his grandfather. The one, despite his every effort, he couldn't get to operate properly. Not on his own.

He had an interest other than boxing, dammit—he just didn't know how to pursue it. Not without branding himself a simpleton.

"Daniel," Elizabeth called his attention back to her. "Why can you not find a hobby that doesn't involve being at daggers drawn or going at loggerheads several times a week?"

Feeling instantly defensive, and uncertain why, he sputtered, "I like to bu-bu—" Blast it! He couldn't even get out a simple three letter word: *box*. A fast exhalation and he spit out, "Like sparring."

"You like beating things to a pulp and proving how strong you are."

A pulp? Talk about embellishing!

So he enjoyed a few rounds of pugilistic endeavors every week. Could he help it if he was adept at fighting? If the exhilaration he got from firing off punches and having onlookers cheer him on helped sustain him through the silent—and solitary—hours of his life?

He didn't have to talk in the ring. Wasn't expected to wax eloquent at the boxing academy.

Didn't have to jabber over inane comments that in reality meant nothing. All he had to do was strip off his shirt, strap on his gloves—when he and his sparring partners agreed to them—and let his fists talk for him.

It was the one place he could be around his peers without fearing coming across as weak.

"Men!" A decidedly feminine lift of one shoulder accompanied that pronouncement. "Why you cannot all find tamer amusements closer to home that satisfy your manly urges, I'll never comprehend."

What? Had she been reading his mind?

"What's this?" She noticed the advertisement he'd cut out announcing Mr. Taft's visit to London and presentation on orreries.

Something Daniel had been debating whether or not to attend. "A lecture I'd like t-to hear."

"On what?" She turned the page toward her, then flicked it away with a smile. "Orreries. I should have known. Go. I daresay it'll be a good experience for you." Her gaze drifted across the room. "Have you fixed it yet?"

His scowl answered for him.

"Then go. Learn who else shares your interest. Possibly get Grandfather's machine running again." She gave his face an arch look. "A much better pastime than fighting, if you ask me."

Before he could respond, the bright smile slid from her face. "Daniel. I came because I needed to see how you got on." Her gaze flicked over to the window behind him, then she focused on his face. Her beautiful eyes were somber, sadder than they should be. “I know where your mind tends to dwell on days such as this.”

He wondered whether she knew he was expecting her husband. That he had other, even more pressuring, topics on his mind. As always, when in the company of anyone save Cyclops, he carefully considered his words before he spoke. “Meeting someone shortly. ’T-tis what snares my attention.”

Well, that and Penry’s note.

“Oh, posh.” She dismissed his excuse. “No one ever calls this early.” Elizabeth rose and gripped his clenched fists. He hadn’t realized his fingers were tangled until she applied herself to unknotting them. “When shall you forget all he did?”

He didn’t need named, nor the incident in question. They both knew what had transpired that long ago rainy afternoon. Elizabeth had been so young, Daniel marveled that she still remembered.

God knew he’d never forget. After all this time, it wasn’t what their sire did that haunted Daniel; it was what he’d said.

’Twas barely a year after his twin brother died; David’s sudden absence leaving a gaping hole in young Daniel’s life. He’d just seen Robert, his older brother, and their dear mother put in the ground. A child of nine should’ve been allowed to grieve. But that would have been a luxury in the presence of his austere parent. A parent who had just found Daniel and his sister crying in their mother's abandoned morning room and who quickly made his displeasure known.

Craven bastard. Stop cowering like a whipped cur! It's only a little blood. Father had turned from him then and wiped his riding crop clean while leaving the blood to dry on his only remaining son's face.

"Daniel."

The sound came from far off, far away from the memories gripping him. *Not a day goes by I don't wish you'd expired instead of them. Sodding Fate—took me wife and real sons and left me a useless cripple! The revered Tremayne title, going to a bloody idiot—it makes me sick.*

"B-but, Father," he'd stammered, as he had for years, "you du-du-don't mean—"

Damn imbecile! His sire had rounded on him, crop slashing toward his head for another strike. *You are dead to me, do you hear? Dead to me!* The blows fell swift and accurate, piercing his heart and shredding confidence more than skin, slicing will more than flesh. *Dead! To! Me! Some fiendish plot of Satan may have saddled me with his stuttering spawn, but you will not speak in my home. Ever, ever again!*

Warm fingers plied at his neckcloth, stroked his cheeks. "Daniel. Come back to me, dearest. Daniel!"

The terror receded under the heartfelt pleas of his beloved sister. His arm came round her, and Daniel was startled to find himself standing in the middle of his study with no recollection of having moved there.

"Ah, Ellie, I am... Fine." When she would have gone on smothering him, he pulled her hands down and set her away. "Fine now, thanks to-to-to you."

She gripped his wrist when he tried to escape toward his desk. "What has happened?" Her grasp tightened and she forced him to face her. "What has changed? You've not—not..."

Humiliated, he spun from her hold to finish bitterly, "Not acted the madman?"

"You are not and never were," she cried. "And that wasn't what I meant to say!"

"Acted the-stupid-clunch?" Without thought or intent, the words rushed out, angry bullets peppering the air. "Buffle-headed-chaw-bacon-nnnnnn—" *Noddy!* If his tongue hadn't glued itself to the roof of his mouth, who knew how long he might have gone on spewing self-directed insults? Insults he'd heard time and again from both Robert and his father.

"Not *retreated*." Elizabeth said it as though he'd gone on a mere vacation, a weekend sojourn, when in fact he knew the lapses frightened her. Damned if they didn't frighten him too. Which probably explained, if not excused, his anger. It had been years since he'd lost the present like that, fled inside himself to escape the taunts. "You've not retreated in so very long. Why now? What has happened?"

"I've not been sleeping well," he admitted, startled when the truth slid from his tongue with such ease. "Not sleeping much at all. Not since pa-pa-

parting ways with Louise and— D-damn me! I should not have said *that* to you."

Red crept over her sun-tinted features, rendering her as cherry bright as one of the tomatoes she grew with such pride. "Daniel," Elizabeth chided, and he saw how she busied her hands arranging the folds of her dampened skirt in order to avoid his gaze, "lest you forget, I am a married woman now. I daresay you may speak of your...your paramours without any fear of censure from me."

Bemused by her attempt at sophistication, he was nevertheless taken aback when she added, "As to that, if you cannot sleep for the lack, though how one could miss that coarse wretch I cannot fathom, then why not simply find another?"

A single time, well before her own recent marriage, Elizabeth had visited London and stumbled upon him and Louise during one of their rare public outings. A new Egyptian exhibit had opened and apparently both women had fancied seeing a mummified cat. Likely the *only* thing his sister and former mistress shared in common, given how Elizabeth possessed elegance and sweetness and the most tender of hearts, qualities the self-serving, sometimes crude, always lusty Louise could never hope to attain.

"You'd recommend I find another coarse wretch t-to warm my bed?" He didn't try to halt his chuckle at her look of outrage.

"Never that, you wicked fiend!" She swept up her frilly parasol and playfully swatted his shoulder with the side. "You are the best of men and deserve only the best of women. Louise could never be that for you and I'm relieved you finally saw it. I do think it's time you found a wife though. Someone to love—"

"A wife? I think not." He cut her off by snaring the pointy end of her parasol. It might not be one of her hair ribbons he'd filched but it would do. He set off, tugging her round the room as he had when they were younger, swerving between furniture, orreries on display and book-lined walls as he steered her toward the exit. The subject of a wife was not one he chose to contemplate, not today. Especially when he'd yet to respond to Penry's note. "Let me amuse myself with at least one fine mistress 'ere I fall upon the bu-bu-*blade* of the parson's mousetrap."

By design, they'd reached the door of his study. Daniel nudged it open and waved for the remaining footman to summon her maid from the kitchens before he turned back to Elizabeth, who frowned up at him.

"What?" he asked, their laughing trek around the room loosening his tongue. "And why are you shredding me with that affronted look? I cannot indulge in a bit of b-bachelor fare before I am no longer one?"

"'Tis not that. 'Tis—"

"Ah. Tremayne." The masculine voice interrupted whatever she'd planned to say. "Your good man Rumsley told me to come right up and here I find you entertaining my lady wife."

A grin broke free and Daniel released the parasol to take the outstretched hand of his brother-in-law.

"Wylde. You made it." An hour overdue. And looking a mite haggard. Odd, that. "Glad to see the latest storm d-d-"—*didn't*, dammit—"failed to carry you off."

"Wylde." Her demeanor subdued, Elizabeth gave her husband a deferential curtsy.

"My lady." Wylde's bow was just as restrained. "I did not expect to find you here."

The formal greeting between the pair wasn't anything unusual. Nor was the flush on her cheeks—Elizabeth pinkened over the slightest provocation. But the sudden anger glinting from her expression? The hard clench of Wylde's jaw when he addressed her? His unpolished appearance, coat buttons askew? Those were definite surprises.

"And I did not realize visiting my brother was disallowed."

Daniel's brows flew skyward at that. It wasn't his place to inquire into the married lives of others but still... "Is all well...between you?"

Elizabeth flashed teeth and eyes at him. Hazel eyes that shimmered with unshed emotion. "Lovely. And now, I'm off. The house does not run itself you know. Oh wait." She cast a cutting look toward her husband. "It does! How juvenile of me to forget."

With an uncharacteristic flounce, she whirled toward the stairs.

"Pardon me," Wylde said swiftly. "I need a word with my wife." He sped across the landing. "Elizabeth!"

Backing into his study, Daniel left the door ajar

so he could observe. Trusted friend or not, if Wylde was mistreating Elizabeth, Daniel wouldn't stand for it. But though he witnessed a heated exchange, one that lasted well beyond a "moment", and though he hated the growing look of horror on his sister's face the more Wylde talked—low murmurs indistinguishable at this distance—Daniel couldn't miss the passionate kiss his friend bestowed on her or the powerful way Wylde captured his wife when, at its conclusion, she would've tumbled down the stairs.

Neither could he miss how Wylde ensured she found her balance, then stood stoically with nary a flinch when she steadied herself and delivered a stinging slap to his cheek. One that rang louder than any syllable of their exchange.

Whatever convoluted emotions presently ruled his sister's marriage, the steely look of determination on Wylde's face as he watched his wife calmly descend the stairs, the man's rigid stance only easing once she was safely on level ground, boded well for an eventual reconciliation. Or so Daniel hoped.

What was that all about?

He retreated to his desk, a mahogany monstrosity he rather favored, and assumed The Pose, the one he'd perfected after analyzing how it made his father so intimidating.

What in blazes was going on with his normally refined friend? The man was always in twig, never such a shabbaroon. Saved from being a dandy by his posture and bearing alone, Wylde spent an inordinate amount of time on his grooming—but not today. Mayhap his valet had quit, beleaguered by the stringent demands of his employer? Daniel's lips quirked at the thought. Wylde had to dress himself and that was why he was late?

An inch or so shorter than Daniel, Wylde nevertheless often appeared taller, being more leanly built. But though the brushed-back dark hair was typically styled to Byronic perfection, today it had the look of stress and sleep.

Wylde returned to the study and shut the door to prying ears. When he turned, Daniel pounced. Arms spread wide, fingertips perched on the surface, upper body inflated and bowed forward, head leading the charge, he roughly inquired, "Wylde? Is there something you want...to...tell me?"

The imprint of fingers flared bright on his friend's surprisingly stubbled cheek. "Nay."

Daniel bristled and abandoned the stupid pose to stand. Once the din made by his chair toppling behind him died to an echo, he growled, "T-try again."

A sardonic lift to his lips, Wylde nodded once. "I may not *want* to tell you anything, but I am *willing* to tell you this: I chose Elizabeth for my bride. Despite what she may claim to the contrary, it is not a decision I regret." Wylde brought one hand up to his cheek, the first acknowledgment Daniel had seen of the impetuous slap. "Although, judging by what you just witnessed and I'm still enjoying"—he fingered the reddened skin—"she derides my methods, I assure you I only seek to garner a satisfying and enjoyable union between us."

Which all sounded well and good but told him positively nothing. "That is all you care...to say?"

"It is."

If there was one thing Daniel had taught himself, it was the art of silence. He employed it now. Occupying himself setting his chair to rights and settling his frame, casually, back into it, he quietly bided his time.

Wylde was here to get something from him—a political issue wasting away in committee he wanted brought to a vote and sought support for, according to the impassioned note he'd sent round yesterday. In fact, he'd requested the ultimate sacrifice: for Daniel to speak—*voluntarily*—in public.

Hell, his prized orrery languished, broken, because he couldn't face a roomful of mechanically minded men discussing their solar system miniatures with relish and great delight, not without revealing himself as a cork-brain the first time he tried to join in, yet Wylde wanted him to make verbose on a topic he could legitimately profess ennui over?

He'd sooner show an asteroid his arse.

Since true friendship was worth personal sacrifice, he'd consider granting the favor. But, gad, the thought of it made his flesh crawl with syllable-spewing maggots.

Before they discussed it further, Daniel expected answers. Ones that explained the strife he'd just witnessed. Perhaps accounted for Wylde's unheard-of appearance.

So he held his peace. Waited.

And without a word, gained what he needed—at least in part—when Wylde, minutes sooner than Daniel had anticipated, exploded with, "To stop you from breathing fire, because a blind man could see you're about to erupt, I'll share this—where it concerns Elizabeth, I believe she and I both want the same result, to make a go of our marriage. More than a tolerable go if I have my way, but we have decidedly different ideas on how to proceed. Thus far I've tried things her way and I don't need to tell you it hasn't proved successful. Now it's my turn." His decisive speech faltered to a musing, "She doesn't like to speak up much, does she? Share what's going on behind those expressive eyes? Like you in that regard but for different reasons, I gather."

Wylde was one of a select few outside his sister who knew of Daniel's ongoing difficulties. "Few" as in two—Penry being the other.

"She wasn't allowed," Daniel conceded. "Not while Father was alive." Not after their mother died. The tyrant who'd created them hadn't wanted to hear a single peep from either of his remaining offspring once the one in his image perished.

"I suspected something of the sort. Tell me—other than dirtying her hands with her prize-winning produce, what might she like? Something she's always wanted to do here in London." Wylde scrubbed one hand down his face and Daniel couldn't miss the lines testifying to sleepless nights. Seemed they had more in common than he'd suspected. "I tell you, I'm at a loss. She's decried attending every ball or *soirée* almost since we came to town. Afternoon carriage excursions in the park are out because she must be home for callers. Morning rides are met with a sniff because the abandoned patch of garden needs to be readied for planting and heaven forfend she trust one of the servants to do it for her."

"A sniff? That...does not sound like Ellie." Especially considering how much she loved to ride.

"Laugh not over my husbandly peril, for I tell you I've tried everything I can conceive." Wylde took an impatient step forward, made a fist and slammed it into the opposite palm. "We got on well enough in the country, by blazes! It's only since our return to London that she's turned up stiff."

"Theater?"

"She declined that as well." And the exhalation following that admission said more than words that Wylde had neared the end of his tether. "Have you any other ideas? Any at all? I refuse to strip to skin and prance naked through the furrows she's creating but I fear 'tis coming to that."

The fist landed on Daniel's desk this time. "Stop laughing, damn you! My marriage is not a jest."

Nay, but the thought of his fastidious friend frolicking in the dirt—in his altogether—was. "Hold." Daniel raised his hand, asking for time.

After several moments' silent contemplation, he suggested, "The opera."

"She's already refused."

"T-take her anyway."

Once, when they were children and their parents returned from an evening out, not long before their mother and Robert died, Daniel and four-year-old Elizabeth had watched from behind the balustrade on the second landing, their stuffy older brother off on his own. When Mama had waved to them behind Father's back as he loudly proclaimed he'd never again waste his time attending another loathsome performance, the two had stifled giggles. As always, when Father grumped about, Mama attempted to pacify the ogre, her sincere words complimenting the singers and majestic show drifting sweetly up the stairs and causing little Ellie to vow in a whisper, "I declare, the op'ra must be the most splendid thing in the whole world."

"Aye," he'd agreed, "Mama always has loved the op-p-pera."

Then Elizabeth had turned to him and promptly asked what it was.

He laughed at the memory. Upon becoming the marquis two years ago, he'd purchased a box for the very same reason—to honor his mother. And he'd yet to use it, even once. "Take Ellie," he said now, "and use my...box." When Wylde started to protest again, Daniel sliced his arm through the air. "T-trust me. Have you attended together?"

"Nay."

"Then that is the magic you seek. Now come." A deep breath, then, "Tell me of this"—*blasted*—"issue you wish me...to speak for. What and when?" Perhaps he could manage to come down with a bang-up case of severe laryngitis on the day in question?

"Are you quite positive about the opera? Is there not something else—"

"Have you...been?" Damn. He could feel the muscles in his neck and jaw tightening with the effort to talk without faltering. And this was a casual meeting with one of his closest friends.

Aye, but it follows Elizabeth's unexpected visit and wholly unanticipated mention of marriage. It follows Penry's note, your own thoughts of taking a new mistress, two months of sporadic sleep and the worst lapse you've had in years. It also follows almost seeing your sister tumble down the stairs because a sweeping kiss knocked her off balance—or, more likely, her own reaction to said kiss.

Pah! Excuses, one and all.

How was he to get on in public without coming across as a sapskull? How would he get on *tonight*? Gad. Why could he not simply order up a fulsome wench (one whose wattles didn't hear would do nicely) to present herself in his bedchamber? Have her ply sweet words and warm fingers along his lonely shaft?

While that image might have tightened another part of his anatomy, it did relax his neck. Willing his teeth to unclench and his tongue to cooperate, he clarified, "Been together?"

"What? I'm not following you."

No surprise, as he'd bumbled about long enough. Fortunately, unlike those who sometimes tried to finish his sentences for him, Wylde had the wherewithal to wait patiently, regardless of situation or circumstance, and allow Daniel to find his own way, his own words. "The opera. Have you...with Ellie? Ever?"

"If you'll recall, this is our first joint trip to London. I've never really had the opportunity to take her much of anywhere." His face picked up a degree of animation that had been missing since his arrival. "I'd originally planned to shower her with numerous outings. I'd thought to surprise her, But that was before..." Wylde's features froze into a frustrated mask. "Never mind. Just tell me what to do."

"Trust me. Regard-d-*less* of what she claims, she wants to...go." He'd give it a few weeks and see if things turned, if Elizabeth appeared happier and not just resigned with her marriage before demanding more of an explanation. "Now. About this speech you want me to sputter through..."

"You look like a damn Scot." Wylde jumped on the new topic with relish, coming closer to sink into the very chair Elizabeth had occupied a short while ago.

A slice of sunlight beamed past Daniel's shoulder and onto his desk, bright and cheery. The clouds had moved on then, the sky clearing. Might he hope the remainder of his day was to follow? His fingers went to the bristle covering the bruise. "What of it?"

"You'll have to carve that scruff off your face before you speak."

That was the least of his concerns. "And if I... don't acquaint my jaw with the sharp edge of a razor, what then?" *Am I to be exempt from showing myself to be a bumblehead?*

Assuming the whiskers in question would be gone as advised, Wylde took several folded sheets from his pocket and slid them across the desk. "This covers the salient points and history of the matter. It also highlights what I hope you'll vocalize."

"When?"

"The vote is scheduled for next week. Tuesday afternoon, but I'll have to check to confirm the time—"

"I have plans Tuesday next."

Wylde gave a bark of laughter. "We both know you never have plans."

While that was generally the case, Daniel was tempted to shove the advertisement under Wylde's nose. So much for debating the merits of concealing his idiocy versus his desire to hear a man he respected speak on a topic he adored.

Damn. It looked as though Fate had made the decision for him.

Daniel turned to the last page Wylde had supplied and scanned the summary section. It looked like some rot about escalating crime and city patrols.

If he practiced each line a few thousand times, then maybe...

"I've kept them as succinct as I could," Wylde cajoled. "Just take your time, speak deliberately as you always do and I daresay you'll do fine. It'll be over in a trice."

"I still d-d-don't fathom why you or Harrison can't speak for this. Keep me out of it save for the vote." He could promise to show for that, surely. Though he'd inherited his father's seat on the committee along with the title, he'd yet to attend a single meeting. It appeared his cowardice had finally caught up with him.

"Except for your prowess in the ring and your long-standing association with Louise, you're an unknown. If you show up and make a case for this, I'm betting the obstinate pig-heads will listen. Besides, Harry has his hands full with the corn regulations and we both know I have no reputation to speak of."

"I wonder why," Daniel muttered with unmistakable sarcasm. It was no secret that Wylde had left two women standing at the altar. Daniel didn't know the circumstances surrounding the jilts but Ellie did. When Wylde had come sniffing after Elizabeth, once their father was gone and the proper mourning period observed, she'd demanded an explanation before agreeing to his suit. Daniel had left them alone so Wylde could make it.

"Sodding politics!" Wylde exploded. "I only volunteered to serve on this damn committee so I could gain an audience with your father and plead my case for Elizabeth's hand." *That* was news. "The lobprick squashed my hopes in that regard just as he squashed this bill time and again. And now I've come to care—"

"He chaired the commit-t-tee?"

"For years," Wylde grated out.

His father had been *against* this bill? And now Wylde was giving him a chance to *support* it? Knowing that made all the difference in the world.

Daniel waved his arm, indicating the pages Wylde had prepared. "I'll study."

As though Wylde didn't sense Daniel's capitulation, he continued trying to sway him. "I'm set to chime in the moment you've said your piece and a number of others are lined up as well, but we're still in the minority. Too many stubborn, stodgy old codgers hanging on to their old and outdated ways. But we just might be able to turn the tide this time. Every voice will count."

That's what I'm afraid of. Too bad his had betrayed him since birth.

Wylde stood. "Whatever you do, don't be late."

Daniel grimaced. Of course he was going to be late.

He was always late. One of the subtle ways he'd found to avoid people. And especially conversations.

2

TO BE OR NOT TO BE...A FALLEN WOMAN

"Ah, Mrs. Hurwell, I trust we won't be toppling into any displays today?"

Dorothea Hurwell's companion, who had followed her across the threshold in time to hear the churlish greeting, turned to the clerk manning the bookseller's entrance. "Ah, Mr. Tumson," Sarah cooed back in a sickeningly sweet voice Dorothea knew didn't bode well, "I trust we don't mean to be an obsequious toad? Especially toward someone who indulges in her love of books exclusively at your establishment?"

"Indulges?" The prissy man sniffed, giving Dorothea a nasty smirk as she struggled to close her dripping umbrella—and struggled to resist the urge to gouge the pointy end into the unsuspecting anatomy between his legs. "When she's only indulged in buying *one* book in all the time I've worked here?"

Poised as ever, Sarah efficiently closed her own umbrella without ever taking her eyes off the man. Their unusual color and shape—a stormy grey and uptilted at the outer corners—was rather captivating, and at the moment, the clerk appeared completely snared. "I was speaking of myself, for a slight to anyone I'm with cuts deeper than one aimed at me alone. And we both know I have a predilection toward collecting a positively *obscene* number of books. Now, mind you locate some manners the next time you see us or I'll see to it your subsequent task is locating another position. Are we understood?"

He blanched. "Aye, Ms. Vinehart. My apologies, Mrs. Hurwell." A politely subdued nod to each of them preceded his hasty backward retreat. Right into the downpour.

Dorothea muffled a laugh as he scrambled to circle the customer who'd just wrenched the door open against the flailing winds that had plummeted the temperature in the last hour. "Fitting," she murmured when the rude clerk faltered on the slick cobblestones. "I daresay, that's what he gets wasting time maligning me when he should have been manning the door as assigned."

"You have the right of it," her companion agreed, straightening the fingertips on her gloves. "I vow, if he had any more unwarranted airs, he'd float off like a giant balloon."

"If you'd be so kind as to bottle some of your aplomb, I do believe I'd scrape together the funds to buy it," Dorothea told her sincerely, fisting her chilled fingers in their threadbare gloves around the umbrella handle. "Thank you for coming to my defense."

Having anyone stand up for her, since her dear mother departed decades too early, was such a novelty Dorothea never failed to notice and appreciate.

"Would that it weren't necessary." That she hadn't fallen on such dire times. But alas, every day was a new opportunity—and one step beyond the smothering silence imposed by her now-deceased spouse. She felt her lips curved in a rueful, embarrassed quirk. "Or that I could defend myself so ably."

"Think nothing of it." Sarah surveyed the ground floor of Hatchards Booksellers. The murky weather had driven a fair number of people indoors, far more than they typically saw this early in the day. "It's too crowded down here. Shall we explore the upper floors?"

Knowing that their presence in the shop was due to its convenience as a meeting place much more than either's desire to select reading material—at least this particular morn—Dorothea gave her umbrella one last shake before placing it in the bucket set aside to collect the abundance of drips. "Of a certainty, let's."

Of medium-to-short height (Dorothea always preferred to put the "medium" first), her feet traipsed up the stairway swifter than her tall friend, as she took two steps to every one of Sarah's.

Unlike most Thursdays when they casually browsed the latest offerings on the street level while speaking in hushed tones on whatever topics struck their fancy, today it wouldn't do to be overheard.

The second they reached the third floor and found a tucked-away corner, Sarah spun in place, an animated expression brightening her countenance. "There now. With prudent people staying out of this dog soup of a storm, our privacy should be assured. So tell me," she ordered, her hushed whisper barely disguising her eagerness, as she grasped Dorothea's wrist to pull her closer, "have you sufficiently considered what I proposed last week?"

At the firm pressure on the recently abused skin, Dorothea's breath hissed outward, but she managed not to betray the discomfort any other way.

"Do you not think it the most viable of solutions?" Sarah continued, her delight palpable.

Before Dorothea could formulate a reply—she'd pondered little else!—Sarah released her wrist and liberated a napkin from her reticule. "Here, eat this." She pressed a cube of cheese into Dorothea's thinly gloved palm and popped a smaller portion into her own mouth. "Nay. I don't want to hear a single protest. Don't faint as you did last week, and that will be thanks enough."

The additional reminder of that mortifying experience was sufficient inducement, and the crumbling cheese went down as though it were the smoothest of nectars. "You are too thoughtful."

"And you are too young to be fraught with such difficulties. Now tell me—will you take the next step and come tonight?"

Take the next step and admit she couldn't care for herself? Admit she *needed* a man? A rich one, likely a titled one? A difficult task to be sure, when from Dorothea's limited experience, the male persuasion had very little to recommend it.

"Take a lover, you mean? So I can eat? Does it not seem sordid somehow?" Sordid and immoral? But Dorothea knew better than to disclose that secondary concern, given how her friend *lived* the part Dorothea was only contemplating: the part of mistress, of paid companion. Of courtesan... The part of a lover.

Strange to consider, especially for someone who had, as an adult, never felt *loved*.

"Sordid? Not at all," the elegant and older Sarah assured with complete certainty. "And you're not taking a lover for the thrill, though I do hope he'll give you plenty of those, you're taking on a *protector* if you choose to move forward. And that, my dear, is an entirely different proposition."

Grateful for the tall stacks of books waiting to be shelved in the corner they occupied, Dorothea ducked behind a rather impressive one. Reaching for the topmost book, she buried her flaming face in the open pages and allowed her gaze to fix on the lines of poetry. But she saw only a blur. Every speck of her attention was centered on the woman next to her and the illicitly intriguing idea she proposed.

If Dorothea did this, she'd become some man's mistress, possibly by morning. If she didn't, she might as well die because dramatic or not, that was where things were heading. She couldn't go much longer without regular nourishment. Not and have the strength, or will, to fight off her grabby landlord and his unsavory advances.

"I..." Dorothea swallowed the stone that had taken up residence in her throat and quickly turned another page. Still focused on the thin volume shielding her face, she said, "I believe you may have the right of it. Lord knows everything else I've tried has failed to yield results. But how does one not versed in the trade go about finding a suitable protector?" Go about *satisfying* one, she really wanted to ask.

Dorothea had no illusions about her attractions. She had no station, no dowry, no claim to any particular talent—other than a keen interest but unremarkable ability on the pianoforte, an instrument her genteel mother had only just begun teaching her young "Thea" shortly before succumbing to a wasting disease.

How was Dorothea—a woman born of an earnest but impoverished shipping clerk, long since deceased, and wedded to a shopkeeper without any aspirations, more recently deceased—supposed to secure a wealthy patron?

"Mr. Hurwell was the only man I've endured intimate relations with," she admitted in a small voice, rapidly turning pages to fan her heated face, "and our physical relations were..."

Lacking. Disappointing. Sometimes painful.

A cultured female hand eased into view and obliterated the unrecognizable words shimmering before her eyes. Seconds later, the book slid from her grasp when Sarah determinedly took possession. "Dorothea, child, look at me."

At twenty-six, she was hardly a child, but she did as bade. "You must think me incredibly gauche. I know you only seek to help. Why can I not claim your poise and confidence? The mere thought of attempting to entice a man with this"—Dorothea's empty hands gestured to what she considered a less-than-enticing form—"churns my insides like cream into butter."

Sarah's smile was a balm. "You do have my poise, if you would but believe it. All women have it within themselves to feel confident and beautiful."

Dorothea couldn't help the snorted, "*All* women?" that escaped.

She was plain and skinny and she had no qualms admitting either. Her landlord Grimmett accused her of both and did so with increasing frequency, deriding how she'd likely not find a better offer. Offer? Was that how the weasel described forcing his attentions? And Mr. Hurwell? During the entirety of their eight-year marriage, her husband had naught positive to say on her looks. Or anything else for that matter, insisting the female mind was not adapted to troubling itself with conversation or concerns beyond the home.

Bah! She'd rather not waste thoughts on either of them.

"Aye, all women." Sarah's tone brooked no argument but it was the conviction shining from her gaze that arrested Dorothea's attention. "And that is a gift the right man can grant."

"A gift? How so?"

"A man who values *you*, your words and intellect." Sarah's eyes took on a luminescent glow. "A man who thrives on your passionate nature, why, he can make you feel the most desired and necessary creature on the planet, no matter that you counted three new wretched wrinkles that very morn. And plucked two chin hairs the night before."

Dorothea bit off a laugh. Sarah may have been fourteen years her senior, but wrinkled and blemished she was not. Though a faint line or two was hinted at beneath her eyes, nary a grey hair peeked from the edges of her bonnet, and she had the kindest, most inviting face Dorothea had ever seen. That was one of the things Dorothea had noticed the moment the two struck up their first conversation the previous year, both waiting in line to inquire about the latest Miss Austen book, *Mansfield Park*.

Regretfully, that splendid story was the last time she'd had funds to fritter over something as trivial as reading. But purchased or not, books were usually free to browse, and thank goodness for that, because she continued to cross paths with Sarah.

Mere weeks later, after they'd crossed paths by sheer coincidence an amazing six times, and enjoyed more meaningful conversations with each subsequent meeting, Dorothea had learned of Sarah's profession. Though astonishment threatened to paralyze her lips, curiosity won out and Dorothea, in turn, confided about her own lackluster marriage. A few months later, Mr. Hurwell's fondness for gambling over horse races had made him devastatingly poor—and her a not-quite-devastated widow.

Regardless of what brought Dorothea to this point, the truth was indisputable—Sarah most certainly did *not* look like a woman whose livelihood was dependent upon her ability to seduce men. Warm and friendly, yes. A *coquette?* Not that Dorothea could see.

Could that possibly bode well for her, then? If she were matched with the right man, would she, perchance, inherently possess the ability to seduce?

"There now," Sarah complimented, "you flush prettily. That is all the gentlemen want—a woman to make blush, and one who will want them back."

"But what if I don't?" The unexpected praise emboldened her. Dorothea stood on her toes to confirm that no one browsed nearby. Their seclusion assured, she voiced one of her fears. "Mr. Hurwell never dwelled overmuch with things in the amorous realm." That was an understatement. "But I sincerely doubt a man who is arranging his pleasures beforehand so they are conveniently available at his whim wants them from a cold stick with no sultry talent or sensuous airs."

"A cold stick?"

Dorothea waved it off as she would a pesky fly. "Oh, bother it. I should not have said that."

"Who *did* say that?" Sarah's tone stated she'd brook no evasion.

Dorothea escaped toward another tower of books.

Books, soothing books, with their familiar-smelling pages, their comforting lines of text. They didn't ridicule or belittle. They didn't snatch dreams away and replace them with soul-stifling monotony. They didn't scare or intimidate. Nay, books, and the words that comprised them, inspired and remained Dorothea's one escape.

"Who?" Sarah persisted.

But not today, it seemed. "Just Grimmett. Something he said yesterday when he came to collect the rent." Grimmett *and* her husband, when he'd been alive.

Sarah moved swifter than a hawk and captured Dorothea's right wrist. "Is that all he managed to collect?" Her fingers whispered across the splash of betraying color on Dorothea's wrist not quite hidden by the ragged lace.

Though she tried, Dorothea couldn't quell the pressure increasing behind her blinking eyes. "Dorothea. Today is not the first time you've worn bruises where bracelets belong. He's becoming more aggressive, isn't he?"

At that, the first useless tear edged free despite her vain efforts to will it back.

"You *cannot* allow yourself to remain— Oh, dear, and now I've made you cry! Blast me, I did not mean to rouse uncomfortable thoughts. Forgive me." Sarah pulled Dorothea into her arms for a fierce, almost motherly embrace. "I vow, together, we shall make things right."

Dorothea returned the hug while dashing away the remnants of unacceptable tears. Had she not shed enough last night? And over the last two months when her funds depleted to nearly nothing and her efforts at finding employment continued to yield the same?

Sarah eased her hold and Dorothea stepped back. She quickly tugged her sleeve down, muffling a curse when the tattered edge tore. "He is getting rougher, I admit. But I dispatched him soon enough."

"Soon enough to protect your virtue, mayhap, but not the growing fear."

Feeling trapped, Dorothea raised stark eyes to Sarah. "But what if he's harsh or cruel?"

"Grimmett? Hasn't he already been?"

"No, I mean my new protector, assuming one is to be found. What if I fail to please *him* and he punishes me for it, and I've nowhere else to turn because he *owns* me? My home, my attire. Will I be at his mercy? Have I any right to gainsay him?" In truth, this mistress business seemed far more complicated than starving. More frightening on some levels, too. "Or am I being jingle-brained?"

Sarah's laughter brightened their book-warmed corner. "Come now, I talk not of selling your soul to the devil or your body to an ogre. You're still free to say yea or nay, always and with any man." She leaned close and whispered under her breath, "I concede there are vile men walking London and some may very well be in search of a mistress, but not in *my* circle. The people I would introduce you to are known to me, be assured. Please, dither no more. Agree to come to the dinner party tonight and decide for yourself after you meet the man I think could answer all your prayers."

"Oh? You've invited the Almighty?" she somehow managed to jest. "I didn't know He possessed a fondness for turtle soup."

"You wretch!" Sarah chided, but some of the worry shading her gaze fled. "Do come. Penry and I have put our heads together these last weeks and truly think we've found you a perfect match."

"You've discussed me with your... With Lord Penry?" Sarah's longtime protector was married with five daughters, but in the time she and Dorothea had been friends, Sarah had never indicated Dorothea might warrant being a topic between them.

"We have, dearest. From the moment I realized you were in dun territory and all alone, without—"

"I have my mice, don't forget."

Sarah tightened her lips against a smile but continued speaking. "All alone and struggling in your attempts to find a workable solution to your predicament."

Ah, yes. Her predicament—widowed and penniless.

Without tact or fanfare, Dorothea had swiftly learned young women lacking practical experience or applicable references (actually, lacking any references at all) were shown the door of respectable establishments faster than the overhead bell could chime *adieu*.

The meager resources remaining after Mr. Hurwell's inhospitable cousin had claimed the shop —and, by right, her living quarters above—had dwindled to a pittance since her eviction. As the only child of two only children, therefore having no family in London and no other viable choices that she could discern, Dorothea had perfected the art of frugal, solitary living. (She didn't think one-sided discourses conducted with George and Charlotte counted; their whiskers might bob and tails twitch, but as conversationalists, they left much to be desired.)

Yet Sarah spoke of meaningful discussions. How that beckoned to someone who longed for true companionship over and above that of a bursting table. "He talks with you, your Lord Penry? About his day and such? How often does he come round?"

Dorothea knew Sarah's benefactor paid for her lodgings and kept her flush in the pockets, and that Sarah readily traded her body in exchange for the security of her living. But never before had she considered how the two might be *friends*. A mere mistress and a lofty lord. It was an unexpected, exhilarating concept. One that tempted.

"Of a certainty we talk." Surmising Dorothea had warmed to the idea, Sarah's stance relaxed. "We touch upon everything: his day, mine, interesting *on dits*, what event to attend or host next, Prinny's latest foibles, political issues facing—"

"What about Lord Penry's family? His wife?" The words wouldn't be contained. "Do you speak of her? Forgive me if it's impertinent to ask, but I truly desire to know. I mean, what are the boundaries of such a union? How does one avoid crossing them?"

A flash of sadness swept across Sarah's eyes, and then it was gone. "Nay. We do not speak of his wife and only rarely his daughters. But on other topics, I have free rein. As to you and your protector, simply let him set the pace. Like a horse to bridle, you follow his lead. Don't frown at me like that—have you not seen how the men of the ton treat their horseflesh?"

True. So true. Mr. Hurwell had wasted every spare farthing attending—and wagering on—horse races, no matter that the man had never set atop one and professed no eagerness to try.

"But for now," Sarah continued, "when I have a particular someone in mind, you may set *your* mind at ease for he is most certainly a gentleman, one with nary a vile rumor attached to his name."

That brought Dorothea up short. She'd thought

Sarah had been jesting earlier when she mentioned selecting someone. "You have?"

"Of a certainty. A marquis, in fact."

A marquis? The mere possibility sent her mind spinning in a disorderly bustle. Yet Dorothea managed to respond, with a lack of sputtering she thought impressive indeed, "Perhaps you aim too high on my behalf?" Thanks to her mother's tutelage, Dorothea knew how to conduct herself and speak with more refinement than many in her class, but she had no right to or expectations of such grandeur. "Would not a second or third son or perhaps a merchant with heavy pockets not be more suited—"

"You measure your worth in drams when you should be thinking in barrels." Sarah sniffed as though Dorothea's concept of a more appropriate protector was preposterous. "Whatever notions you have of unsuitability, discard them henceforth. You exhibit as much grace as any number of other women of my acquaintance and your manner is more pleasing than most. Once you're able to fill your belly regularly, I daresay your countenance will rival that of anyone's. Cease doubting, dear. I would never seek to place you in a situation that would cause you to wish for the gallows."

"I know that, I do. I'm just..." Dorothea's faltering dance toward another stack of books spoke for her. A tiny part of her was fascinated by the very real prospect of enjoying a man's companionship. And if, in turn, he enjoyed her body, then what would be the harm? She groped for something to occupy her hands and reached for the nearest book.

Sarah intercepted her efforts and pressed her palms against Dorothea's restless fingers. "Beset by nerves. 'Tis understandable, so let me tell you more of what to expect so you'll feel as snug as a duck in a ditch."

"Let's hope it's not raining then, for the duck's sake." She squared her shoulders and faced her fate head on. "All right. Tell me the worst of it."

Sarah raised a beautifully arched brow. "Since you put it that way... Tonight's party is at my home. Several of us rotate hosting duties and it is my turn for the chore. There will be approximately a dozen men present and an equal number of women. Women who, by choice or circumstance, are in the business of physically pleasing members of the ton. Several will come with their benefactors; others are looking to make new associations. Others only want to dabble and play for the night. There will..."

Sarah paused as though weighing whether or not Dorothea truly wanted to hear more.

Of course she did! This was a slice of life she'd never anticipated finding herself nudging up against. "What else? Do tell me everything so shock won't send me swooning out the door."

With a comforting pat, Sarah released her hand. "Good girl. I do believe you'll do fine. Since everyone knows tonight is about partnering and pleasuring, either for the evening or beyond, don't expect restraint. While some couples prefer to take themselves off before offing their clothes, others aren't as circumspect."

Dorothea felt her eyes go wide. "I'll be expected to *undress*?" The question squeaked higher than the roof two floors above. "In front of everyone?"

"Most certainly not! But others may and you did say you wanted to know the worst. I'm sure you can ascertain what might come next from any pairs, or groups, who are so inclined."

Groups?! It was a wonder her face hadn't ignited.

In order to speak, Dorothea had to unlock her teeth, which had mashed the insides of her cheeks. "Are you quite certain this is the proper venue for me to meet this man? Would it not be"—*safer for my sanity*—"easier were we to meet elsewhere?" Mayhap at church?

"Ah, would that it were that simple. Lord Tremayne rarely accepts social invitations, especially now that he's seen his younger sister married off. He's not a man given to idle chatter from what I've seen. Prefers meaningful discourse to those of the flittering masses. Penry said we accomplished quite a feat, securing his agreement to attend tonight."

Lord Tremayne. What a strong-sounding name. Dorothea wondered whether his character might be strong as well. In truth, she wondered whether his *body* might be, and her face flamed hotter. "Why did he?"

"To meet you, of course."

"But I... I haven't even agreed to come. And he knows nothing about me."

"Ah, but we knew he was in the market for a new mistress and Penry is one of his oldest friends, so when he mentioned you, Tremayne listened."

"So they're of the same age?" Penry was a year or two older than Sarah; she'd let that tidbit slip one morning when she'd arrived at Hatchards late, hurried and flushed, commenting that the man's stamina wasn't waning with his recent birthday (and appearing rather pleased by the prospect).

"Nay. Tremayne is younger by ten years or so." Sarah gave a saucy wink. "So he's in his prime too. Very fit. Taller than most, and strong."

"Heavens, Sarah, it sounds as though you're describing a circus bear, not a man."

Her friend's grey eyes sparkled. "I daresay you'll find much to admire about him. As to tonight's gathering, dearest, do keep in mind that meeting him in such a setting ultimately protects you both."

"Protects? From what?" All sorts of dastardly thoughts pelted her.

"You silly pea goose—protects your *pride*. Watch." Sarah slipped two books off a nearby stack and held them up, covers pressed together. "It's a simple matter to engage each other as much or as little as you choose. If either of you aren't interested in pursuing an association, you simply walk away." Holding one in each hand, she whipped the books apart. "It's as uncomplicated as that. Whereas if you were meeting for a *tête-à-tête*, awkwardness might ensue if one of you felt more inclined to proceed than the other." Sarah slapped the two books together as though to indicate the subject was at an end. "So we're agreed? You'll come?"

"Might he have a pianoforte, do you think?"

"A piano?" Sarah blinked owlishly and Dorothea felt foolish for asking. "My dear, a good man will give his mistress expensive baubles as though they were bags of lemon drops. I'm certain he'll provide you a pianoforte if the two of you decide you'll suit."

With every word she uttered, how was it Sarah made becoming a fallen woman sound more uplifting and enticing? And how did one learn the necessary skills to make a satisfactory go of the venture?

"How does a...a..." Dorothea walled off her nerves and shored up her courage. If she couldn't talk about it, she seriously doubted she'd be able to engage in it. "Mistress behave? In the bedchamber, I mean. And why is it men want a mistress if they already claim a wife?"

After all, she'd been a wife. And from her experience, the occupation had little to recommend it.

"Oh, gracious. Now you're asking questions that go significantly beyond our precious time together. I'm sure there are as many reasons as there are clouds in the sky. An unhappy marriage, an arranged one. A wife who refuses to join her husband in the marriage bed once her duty is done and she's delivered him a son or three. As for those men unmarried, is it not safer—and more expedient—to arrange for a woman you find attractive than risk contracting pox from strumpets on the streets?"

The unsavory aspects of pleasing oneself outside of marriage had not occurred to her. Perhaps because she'd never been much pleased *within* marriage. "You always seem so refreshed. So joyful. As though your time with Lord Penry is not disagreeable. Do you..." Dorothea found her eyes had skittered toward the empty stairwell and she forced herself to meet Sarah's patient expression. "Do you find true enjoyment in the bedchamber?"

Sarah's cheeks pinkened and she looked more like a girl of fourteen than a mistress of forty. "Very much so. It has not always been the case, I confess, with each of my protectors. But I'm very happy with Penry."

And that is when Dorothea made up her mind. Whether this Lord Tremayne indulged in risqué behavior or even told vulgar jokes, whether he changed mistresses as frequently as he did his waistcoats, she'd be a chucklehead not to attempt to find a pleasurable coexistence with such a man. And if not him, then another.

"It will do..." When the words came out hesitant, she cleared her throat and proclaimed with every show of confidence, "I believe I would very much like to find someone as you have. But I admit to fearing I'll not please or satisfy him."

"Lovemaking with someone new is not a race you either win or lose. It's more like...like..." Sarah glanced heavenward, as though casting about for the perfect comparison and hoping an angel would drop it in her mind. She snapped her gloved fingers and looked at Dorothea. "Like crafting the most perfect marzipan. All you need is sugar, almonds and rosewater, but while the basic ingredients might not change from attempt to attempt, the exact amounts and how they're prepared will vary as you tweak and refine your recipe until *voilà*—you land upon perfection, ambrosial bliss upon your tongue. *That's* what perfect lovemaking is all about. The right man knows this and won't expect you to dance on your head the first time you're together. Or even the fiftieth. You'll learn to make your own ambrosia—in your own time." With that unfulfilling explanation ringing in Dorothea's ears, Sarah added, "Have I convinced you? Will you come tonight?"

In the end, the image of dancing on her head while balancing marzipan on her feet was so ludicrous, Sarah's cooking comparison shared so exuberantly, and her own situation so desperate, that Dorothea could do naught but concede. "Aye." Though she might live to regret it, at least she'd live. "I'll be there."

But how? She knew better than to brave walking her neighborhood after dark. Daytime was bad enough.

As though she discerned the reason for the worry on her face, Sarah clasped Dorothea's forearm. "Marvelous. Give me your direction—I'll send a carriage for you at half past six. You'll be the first to arrive and we'll set my abigail to arranging your hair. How does that sound?"

"Thoughtful in the extreme."

"La, 'tis no more than you'd do for me should the situation be reversed. This way, you can be happily ensconced before anyone else makes their bows."

Which meant she had the bulk of the day to press into service her one remaining decent dress. Shore up the seams, make sure above her threadbare gloves the sleeves concealed the bruises without ragged lace falling free, no matter that the dress was hopelessly outdated. "You're too kind. I appreciate all you're doing immensely."

"And I've appreciated your friendship from the moment we met. I only wish I could have done more sooner." With a hand on Dorothea's arm, Sarah steered them toward the stairwell. "You have no idea how relieved I am. I truly think tonight could be the beginning of something wondrous for you. Just like Penry and myself."

Descending the steps next to her friend, Dorothea refused to let the questions beating about her breast take root. Would it be like that for her? Could a cold stick find warmth in the bed of a stranger? And what did it matter that Sarah's "wondrous" man was married—to someone else?

When they reached the ground floor, Sarah indicated the sales counter. "Let me buy you this volume and we'll be off."

"Thank you, but that isn't necessary." Food, she might accept; luxury gifts were another matter entirely.

"Oh, but it is." Sarah brandished the book she'd

slid from Dorothea's grasp earlier. "I see you're a great fan of Byron."

Lord Byron, the gadabout poet. One Dorothea didn't like at all. "But I'm not. Wordsworth and Burns, now *them* I enjoy, but Byron is not a particular favorite. There's no need—"

"There's every need." Sarah fanned the book and two loose pages broke free before she stuffed them back inside. "You proceeded to mangle these and several more when I asked about your landlord. So no more protests. I caused your distress, I owe you reparation."

"You most certainly did not cause my distress. Regardless, Sarah, your friendship repays any debt real or imagined, now and into infinity."

Sarah linked their arms and began making her way toward the clerk. "You're such a dear but I'm still buying you the book. If nothing else, you can use it for kindling."

3

TO CONVERSE OVER DINNER – OR NOT

"DON'T BE HORRIBLY DISAPPOINTED if the food isn't up to expectations."

Sarah surprised Dorothea with that statement when she returned to Dorothea's side in the main parlor after a brief absence in the kitchens—the second absence she'd made in the short time since the splendid carriage had rolled to a stop allowing Dorothea—with the aid of a servant!—to alight.

A carriage she'd been increasingly grateful for, given how the mild but stormy morning had given way to a chilling afternoon, the kind that heralded a bitterly cold night. How she hoped that wasn't an omen for the evening ahead.

"You're bamboozling me," she said now, unable to fathom such a claim, for any meals or snacks served during her prior visits had always been exquisite.

While she'd been to Sarah's residence a few times during the course of their friendship, it had always been during the day and only when Lord Penry was away from town (hence, no chance of his unexpected arrival). Unlike the lurid den of iniquity Dorothea had half expected a "kept" woman to reside in, relief reigned when she found that Sarah's home mirrored her person: tasteful and composed.

"How I wish that I were. Mrs. Beeson quit to keep house for the butcher and his four sons, and finding her replacement has not proved an easy task."

The plump, gregarious woman had been most welcoming to Dorothea—and the extra fare she always insisted go home with their guest had been delicious indeed. "I'll not complain of any food at this point no matter how ill or illustriously prepared, but what of Mrs. Beeson? She left *your* employ to cook for *five men*? Has she more fleas than sense?"

"He gave her his name. She's to mother his boys."

"Ah, then. Happy for her am I."

"I as well. But not for my table." Her rueful expression made Dorothea laugh. "Off with you now. Here's my girl—" Sarah gestured toward the maid skimming down the stairs.

"Miss Sarah." The bright-eyed, mob-capped redhead curtsied at her mistress and then beamed at Dorothea. "Is this your friend?" Without hesitation the girl, who couldn't have been much over sixteen, plucked at Dorothea's freshly washed hair (a luxury she'd indulged in this afternoon, having hoarded what water she could the past few days;

even cold and liable to make her scalp feel like frozen tundra for the two hours it took her hair to fully dry, it had been worth it). "Gah." The girl frowned. "Gettin' this thick mass to take a curl will be a chore, I tell you.

"Don't be sittin' on thorns, none." The girl made shooing motions, urging Dorothea up the stairway. "No time to waste!"

With that, Dorothea was herded into the care of Sarah's capable servant.

Thirty minutes later, declining to don the beautiful dress the servant tried to coax her into—there was no way Dorothea's bosom would have adequately filled the top nor her shorter legs the skirts—but wearing the stunning evening gloves in kid leather that her friend had left boxed and beribboned, she rejoined Sarah as they waited for the remaining guests to arrive.

"What? Not the dress?" Sarah took up her hands, pulling the leather past Dorothea's elbows and smoothing the fingers in place. "The gloves. At least you accepted those, thank goodness."

"They're lovely." And sumptuous and quite possibly one of the nicest things she'd ever received. "I cannot thank you enough."

"No more purple fingers for you, my dear." And no worries that anyone would see the unsightly bruises, either, Dorothea couldn't help but think with relief. "For these shall keep you warm."

Self-consciously, Dorothea raised one hand to the intricate swept-up coils, in lieu of ringlets, that the servant had miraculously substituted in a trice. "I feel so majestic."

And afraid to move her head lest they topple.

"As you should. Besides, you—" Sarah cocked her head, listening, then smiled and fluffed out her skirts. "If I'm not mistaken, I hear the first carriage now. Chin up, Dorothea dear. The food may not be all that is fine but I can promise the evening will be memorable, and after tonight it is my hope you shall worry no more."

But Dorothea did worry, in her peaceful little shadowed corner, lit only by the candles strategically placed throughout the parlor, as she waited and watched each individual and couple arrive.

Nearly two hours later, though she still claimed the same corner, "peaceful" had been replaced by pandemonium. With every minute that droned by, an increasingly apprehensive weight pressed in on her chest as her thoughts tumbled as freely as did some of the women's inhibitions. And clothing on more than one occasion, as gloves had quickly been stripped, even slippers sailed forth—to her utter astonishment.

Regardless of whatever surprising sights her eyes beheld, the thoughts swirling behind them kept circling back to one unmistakable conclusion: Tonight, if all went according to plan, she would officially join the Fashionably Impure.

It was an unsettling thought. One that had only grown in proportion every moment that she remained alone.

Dorothea surveyed the men congregating about Sarah's parlor, feeling as though her rioting stomach was in danger of expelling what little it held. How she was soon supposed to sit down and act engaging during a five-course supper was beyond her. Nerves held her nearly immobile.

Which of these men would be responsible for her imminent placement into the ranks of London's demireps and courtesans? Would it be a young blood, someone with more pence than sense, who sought to buy favors before his title had to buy a wife? Or perhaps an older, more moderate gentleman, one whose paunch preceded his phiz? Although, really, what did it matter what his face looked like, or his body?

As long as he treated her with a measure of kindness, then she'd be significantly better off. In fact, Dorothea consoled herself, would she not be *raising* her consequence—from starving and practically homeless to protected and well fed? In exchange for simply cultivating a pleasing manner and a satisfactory presence in a man's bed...

She could manage that, surely.

"How are you doing?" Sarah asked in her ear, causing Dorothea to start. She'd lost sight of her friend at some point in the last half hour, hostess duties—and her new cranky cook—demanding much of Sarah's time. "Now that most everyone's descended upon us like a swarm of lusty locusts."

"Rather nervous, I'm afraid," she confessed, wringing her hands in front of her to stop their visible trembling. Why hadn't she thought to bring a fan? (Mayhap because she didn't own one?)

In her element, Sarah looked as composed as ever, her lustrous brown hair done up in loose ringlets about her face and her dress fancier than any Dorothea had ever conceived. In a deep emerald-green fabric that fairly shimmered, the elegant dress barely perched atop Sarah's shoulders, leaving much of her upper chest and all of her arms—above her silk gloves—bare. A profusion of tiny diamonds sparkled about her neck, woven into the most intricate necklace imaginable. A few gems even glistened throughout her curls. With her confident air and bedecked in finery, her warm and kind-faced friend became so amazingly beautiful it almost hurt to look at her.

"Would it be horrid of me to shoo you away?" Dorothea asked, thinking how she definitely needed to invest in a fan. Weren't they useful for hiding behind when one became embarrassed? She glanced down to find that the dull olive fabric covering her chest and arms had taken on the cast of chewed peas in the last few minutes. Ugh! "What was I thinking? Next to your glittering presence, I look a veritable dowd."

The dress she'd thought would serve earlier, especially with its new layer of lace at the cuffs (scavenged from her best petticoat), was easily the oldest, most-out-of-date article of clothing in the room. Even the statuary boasted finer attire—a saucy, beribboned hat perched atop a bust of some bearded Greek fellow, though Dorothea was clueless which one. For the first time in weeks, she thoroughly regretted her decision not to accept when Sarah tried to gift her with a new gown. At the time, it had seemed prudent—walking about her neighborhood in finery was the surest way to invite unsavory notice. Now though…

"Dearest." Sarah placed her hands around Dorothea's and spoke earnestly. "It's not your dress he'll be considering. It's what resides beneath it."

After she laughed, Dorothea growled, "Was that supposed to alleviate my discomfort? If so, I'm afraid you've accomplished the opposite for it's looming ever larger." Her anxious gaze skimmed over the men in the room once more. "Which one is he?"

Was Lord Tremayne the portly gentleman in the opposite corner who puffed on a cigar in the presence of the women—which even Dorothea, with her limited knowledge of tonnish proprieties, knew was beyond the pale? He also, she couldn't help but note, patted the bum of every female who passed within arm's distance, encouraging Dorothea to remain right where she was—bum against the wall.

Or was Lord Tremayne the gentleman with absurdly bushy side whiskers? The one who'd been leering at her since he walked in? Or perhaps the fellow with a deep laugh and a nose so large Dorothea feared he'd poke out her eye were they ever to kiss? Or mayhap the gangly youth who stood, unfathomably, off to the side appearing as ill at ease as she felt?

In truth, none of them appealed.

Nor did the other prattling four, just coming in, talking loudly with the equally vivacious women on their arms. Women who were more colorful than any profusion of rainbows—and just as above Dorothea's own meager station. How could she hold her head up among such lovelies? As to that, how did *they* hold their heads up with such thick layers of cosmetics plastered on their faces? And who was she to be thinking such critical thoughts?

"You neglected to tell me rouged lips and kohl-rimmed eyes were a prerequisite," Dorothea said softly. "Really, Sarah, given my dated dress and bare face"—*and complete lack of sexual confidence*—"I'm so very out of place."

"I think you worry overmuch. Pay attention because..." Sarah gave her hands a reassuring squeeze, then turned to wave at one of the heavily made-up highfliers. "By the end of dinner that one will be so in her cups she'll find Socrates amusing." Ah, so that was the identity of the bonneted bust. "And Dominique there"—fingers fluttered toward a raven-haired beauty who returned Sarah's greeting with a cool nod—"her accent will start to slip by the third course. Her manners far sooner."

Hearing of their foibles, some of the tightness eased from Dorothea's frame. "But I thought these women were your friends."

Sarah looked right at her, a piercing glance completely void of the artifice she'd just shown the room at large. "You, my dear, *are* my friend. A select few of these women are as well, but most of them are simply competition. That's how they view me and I them."

"Oh." Some of the thawing nerves inside Dorothea froze, thickened. "That's...sad."

"I know it sounds callous, but that's the way of it. Why do you think I delayed hosting for so long, even though it was my turn ages ago? My time with Penry is limited and I guard it jealously. I do not like having to share him."

How Dorothea hoped she might feel the same toward the unknown Lord Tremayne. "Then why must you?"

"Politics. These gatherings give the men opportunity to debate and, if they are successful, sway others to their way of thinking. It's a select few and they're away from the club where others are waiting to pounce in with their own views or agendas. There's a hotly contested vote coming up in Parliament that Penry feels strongly about. As tonight's host, he has more opportunity to guide the conversation in that direction than he might have otherwise."

"Your duty is done," Dorothea told her, "you've adequately convinced me there's more at stake than my ratty dress."

"Then this should comfort you further—despite the breach in etiquette, I've seated you next to me so assistance is only a whisper away if..." A commotion in the hall brought Sarah's head around. "Appears as though Lord Harrison and Anna made it home in time. Wonderful! She's a true friend—I'll introduce you once Harrison takes himself off. They've just returned from Italy. And would you look at that—I declare, her fancy Italian dress looks as though it's from your wardrobe! Her sleeves are long and the cuffs are just brimming with lace!"

Dorothea laughed outright. "Admirable try. Especially as my wardrobe consists of three pegs in the wall."

"Oh look, they brought Susan," Sarah added when a brightly hennaed young woman bounded in after them. "I believe you'll like her as well. There's not an ounce of artifice anywhere and— Fustian! I knew the last few minutes were too calm to last. I see my new cook frantically motioning. Why he abandons the kitchens instead of sending a servant, I know not. I must be off." Sarah kissed her cheek. "Worry not, you'll do fine."

"And Lord Tremayne?" Dorothea squeaked out hurriedly. "Which one is he?"

Sarah acknowledged her cook, indicated she'd be over in a moment, then scanned the crowd.

Dorothea prayed Sarah would point out someone other than the men she'd particularly noticed. There were others, a small, boisterous group of males lingering across the hall in another room, tumblers in hand, but there were as many or more "ladies" in their midst and not a one of the men had cast so much as an inquiring glance her direction. "I thought you said there were only going to be a dozen men here tonight."

Dorothea's count was up to fifteen at least.

"That's what I thought until receiving Penry's note this afternoon. A few others got wind of our gathering and begged invitations." Sarah took Dorothea's arm and casually strolled until she could see into the next room.

Dorothea tried not to be overly critical, tried to remember what awaited her at home: a moldy potato, mice groats—would that her options proliferated as fast as George and Charlotte's "leavings"—and grabby Grimmett. She tried to be grateful, thankful for the opportunity of tonight. But as she evaluated the men present, the ones not melded at the hips to made-up mistresses already, she had to admit not a one of them appealed to her on the physical level she'd secretly yearned for.

"La, that man," Sarah said finally. "I told Tremayne supper was served at nine and not a moment later. And still he runs late."

Upon realizing none of the unpalatable choices before her were the man in question, a surge of relief swept through Dorothea. Mayhap the tardy Lord Tremayne would appeal after all.

Do you recognize the significance of that? a part of her brain seemed to ask.

He's *late*, some imp emphasized.

Late, something her "late" spouse would never, ever have tolerated. Too easily she could recall the disapproving glares should his breakfast, luncheon, dinner—or heaven forfend, afternoon tea—be placed before him even one second beyond the strike of the hour.

My, oh my, Lord Tremayne was tardy. Dorothea smiled, predisposed to like him already.

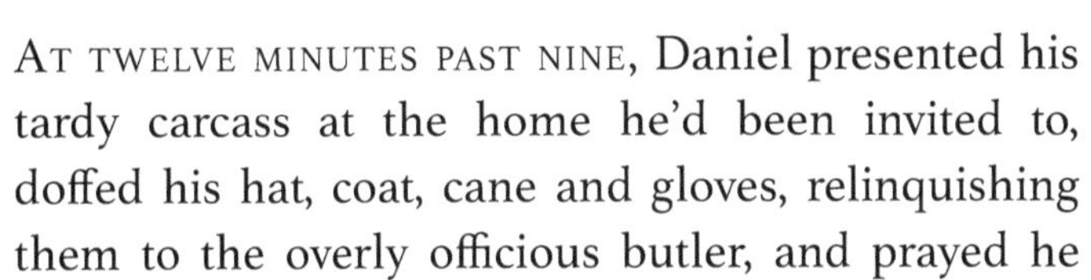

AT TWELVE MINUTES PAST NINE, Daniel presented his tardy carcass at the home he'd been invited to, doffed his hat, coat, cane and gloves, relinquishing them to the overly officious butler, and prayed he hadn't made a mistake in coming tonight.

At the pointedly assessing look the man gave his jaw—insolent fellow!—Daniel's fingers automatically followed. So he encountered scruff instead of skin. What of it? He'd ordered Crowley, his valet, to trim and refine his whiskers in lieu of shaving them off.

Better to disguise the bruise and scars than to scare her away before ever opening his mouth. *Her* being the woman he suffered through this ordeal to meet.

"My lord, delighted you deigned to join us," the butler said with a haughty air that indicated he took his position very seriously. "Dinner is being held on your account, so if you would..."

The man set off at a marching pace before the first syllable of Daniel's "Lead on," made it past his lips.

No out-of-the-way narrow nook for Penry's lovely light-skirt, Daniel saw, the home he was escorted through being as genteel and grand as anything one would expect to find in Mayfair. Only they weren't in

Mayfair, the upper echelon of abodes, but a neighborhood or three away.

"Here we are, my lord."

Nodding his thanks to the impertinent fellow, Daniel paused before entering the formal dining room, keeping out of sight of most its occupants. Though the space was absurdly large, a slightly low ceiling coupled with the crowd inhabiting it gave the room an intimate, almost cozy air. Elaborate candelabra spaced evenly over the table's surface ensured adequate light—a sort of subdued, shadowed light that invited one to lean their head toward their closest companion for a romantic *tête-à-tête.*

He cast his gaze back the way they'd just come and unease threatened to crawl through him. Penry certainly hadn't spared any expense outfitting his mistress, had he?

Daniel hadn't yet seen the lodgings he'd secured for his potential paramour, wanting a fresh start in fresh surroundings with a—hopefully—fresh woman. He'd had his man of affairs take care of it and hadn't bothered to inspect the townhouse himself. Hadn't his man assured him it was just the thing?

The nip of unease promised to metamorphize into an onslaught, fixing him—and his neck muscles in place.

'Tis nothing, he assured himself. Only a willing wren of a widow in need of protection and your pipe in need of her attention. Three fortifying breaths later, he braved crossing the threshold.

Excellent.

Everyone was seated. Just as he'd hoped. Less chance of getting tangled in the trap of idle chatter before supper if people were hungrily anticipating it.

Silently acknowledging the greetings he received from the group at large, Daniel smiled and nodded at several acquaintances as he made his way around the giant oval table to this evening's hostess to make his apologies. He wouldn't put it past Penry to have purchased the huge slab for the occasion—and for the occasion of plowing into his mistress on top of it after everyone went home.

Penry sometimes talked a little too freely about his lusty interludes with the serene brunette. Ready for his own lusty interlude, Daniel scanned the women present, more than a little curious as to the identity of the well-hyped Widow Hurwell.

Penry had teased him with enough hints of subtle beauty and true refinement to pique his interest. But it was hearing of her strained circumstances that had ultimately tipped the scales and caused his carriage wheels to roll this way tonight. No money meant no options, and Daniel was desperate enough in his own right to take advantage of her situation, desperate enough to at least put himself forward. If she was truly as cultured and untarnished as he'd been led to believe, some lucky man would snatch her up and it might as well be him.

"Forgive me," he said to Penry's Sarah, coming up to her and proffering a slight bow, knowing he owed her his sincere apologies for his tardiness but unable to stop himself from avidly inspecting the woman by her side. She was the only female he didn't recognize and the only person who looked more than a little out of place, discounting the pup at the far end who gazed with his mouth agape toward the arched doorway Daniel had just entered through.

In the muted candlelight, she shone like an undiscovered jewel, her wealth of dark hair piled and looped on the back of her head in a manner quite at odds with the simplicity of her dress. But he cared not to analyze her attire for the faint stirring in his loins boded well indeed.

Faint? Putting to rest any concerns he had about not being attracted to her, at the thought of bedding the lovely widow, his body stirred more than a dead man's falling down a ravine—which is what Daniel started to think he'd been for staying with Louise for so long. Dead to any finer sense.

Determinedly, he fixed his gaze on the frowning Sarah. He started to carefully explain his fabricated, rehearsed excuse for being late. His mouth not yet open, already the tension climbed up his neck and squeezed inward—

Not now! he wanted to rail.

But Penry's woman unknowingly saved him.

"Do sit down, Lord Tremayne. I'm grateful you decided to finally grace us with your presence," she told him archly, gesturing to the lone empty seat at the table which, not coincidentally, was next to the woman he had hopes of claiming. "But I've held back supper long enough. Hopkins," she called out to a servant hovering at the ready, "tell Cook the first course may be brought in. *Finally*."

"Yes, madam."

A FRISSON of awareness swelled through Dorothea the moment the latecomer came into view. When Sarah called him Tremayne, the subtle tingling became more of a lightning spike.

Of what, Dorothea couldn't say. The gruff-looking man didn't appeal exactly, but he most definitely *attracted*—both her attention and greetings from many of the men present.

"Glad to see that munsons muffler didn't lay you out for long."

Munsons muffler?

"Nay. Not our man—way to work it till the ringer!"

"Jolly good show, Tremayne."

What? Did he perform in some venue? What an odd occupation for a peer. But apparently, instead of diminishing his standing, it only served to enhance it.

Yet...as he surveyed the room and his gaze alit upon her, she didn't think Lord Tremayne needed any more enhancement when a surge of—

What exactly? Interest? Appreciation? Speculation? A surge of *something* foreign to her experience came into his eyes, something hot and banked glittering from the depths of deep amber. Being the recipient of such focused potency drove some part of her to contemplate jumping from her seat to proclaim she was ready to retire with him straightaway.

The other part of her, the heretofore sensible part that seemed to be undergoing a most peculiar change—into sultry?—commanded her lips to curve into a welcoming smile, her melting body to stay put and her eyes to narrow (she feared losing them if they opened any wider) as he made his way to the available chair next to hers and she undeniably drank him in.

He was a big man, powerfully built yet somehow tamed by the trappings he wore—a rich brown tail-coat over a waistcoat in a muted burgundy stripe, with tan buckskins below. A cream-colored cravat, meticulously tied, and rebelliously straight hair. Rebellious, because all the rage was tousled curls for men and sausage ringlets for the ladies, as she'd been informed when Sarah's abigail had tended to hers.

She liked the silky-looking, thick strands adorning Lord Tremayne's well-shaped head (Mr. Hurwell's had been rather narrow; his head, that was. His hair, somewhat lank.). She liked Lord Tremayne's confident air and strong-looking body too.

She especially liked the way he smelled, now that he was close enough to inhale, clean and spicy, with just a hint of the outdoors.

What she couldn't yet claim to like was his beard.

And how he appeared intimidating beneath the bristle, all hard, flexing jaw and tendon-filled neck—she'd glimpsed a couple inches below his chin and above the cravat when he cocked his head in a peculiar stretch just before taking possession of his chair.

And until she had reason to like *him*, rather than land herself further into the suds, Dorothea knew she'd bide her time. Wait and discern what manner of man he truly was before agreeing to proceed with a liaison between them.

But oh, how she liked the flood of warmth that beset her every limb when he joined her beneath the table, his long, powerful body coming within inches of hers as he brought his chair forward...how she admired his forearm encased in expensive superfine she'd never thought to view up close—much less consider touching, as he reached for his wine...

TAKING advantage of the slight commotion when several servants began tromping in carrying silver-domed trays, Daniel dodged further introductions by settling himself next to the woman he suspected he was here to meet.

And to bed.

Briefly her eyes flicked to his and a ghost of a smile touched her lips before it faded like a breeze. But the damage was done—one covert, up-close, lash-shrouded glance and all he could do was gape and goggle.

Soft tendrils of her luxuriant midnight hair framed a heart-shaped face. The flickering candlelight caused shadows to dance over her slightly angular nose and jaw. She was a mite thin for his tastes, but any hint of hardness in her features was belied by the bow-shaped mouth that commanded his attention.

So easily he imagined those plump lips against his, parted and welcoming, where he would sample the passion he hoped was packaged inside this delightful exterior. He'd like to see her dark hair rid of its pins, his fingers tangled against her scalp as he guided her lips lower...

A hot spike of lust wound through him and Daniel smiled.

Rescuing Sarah's little widow would prove no hardship. Indeed, could the timing have been any more fortuitous? At long last, his long lance would undoubtedly sleep snug and satisfied, and, finally, he'd *sleep*. Snugged against the lithe body he suspected resided beneath the atrocious dress.

Closer now, he couldn't help but notice its shortcomings. Her olive gown had obviously seen better days. A thin fichu was tucked into the low, squared-off bosom, concealing her attributes completely. After the overtly stimulating attire Louise typically wore, the widow's outfit was almost puritan in its severity. Puritan yet provocative...encouraging visions of divesting her of the drab layers and uncovering what lay beneath.

Giving his body a moment to relax, he turned to his meal. A task which proved surprisingly difficult when, moments later, he was fully aware of her slight wrist grappling with the overdone mutton on her plate. His was already neatly severed. So with nothing more than a lift of one brow and an inquiring *Hmmm?* that had her pausing in her efforts, he deftly switched their plates, quickly sliced her serving and had them swapped back before anyone took notice.

A well-timed bite between his choppers ensured all he had to do was nod after her quiet but appreciative thanks and he was off—inspecting her again (for it was a significantly more enjoyable endeavor than chewing overcooked mutton).

A servant came between them bearing gravied asparagus. A particular and unwelcome scent—one he'd suffered enough of thanks to his prior inamorata—wafted strongly from the dish, and Daniel declined.

The man turned to the widow and offered to ladle some on her plate. Daniel watched her nose wrinkle.

"No, thank you," she said quietly. "I'm not fond of onions."

Better and better.

As his eyes skated over her features in profile, another rush of warmth filled his loins. No haggard-looking widow, this, as he'd half feared based on Penry's continued attempts to gauge his interest in Sarah's friend the last week or so. No, this woman looked more like an innocent maiden than a well-used widow.

And just think—if he could deal adequately with the onion-loving Louise for several years, how long might his interest in this divine little morsel last?

"Meezes Hurt-weel, I zee you are new to de trade?" The jewels about her neck as counterfeit as her accent, one of the single females addressed the woman at his side with a bite to her voice. Jealous cat.

"Trade?" his dinner partner queried. "Whatever do you mean?" Thrilled at having her identity confirmed, he was a bit stymied when his widow sounded suitably vague. Was she dense—or only pretending?

"Zee trade of selling *your* wares." With an unmistakable emphasis on "your".

"*My* wares?" Mrs. Hurwell managed to sound both startled and impressed. "You've heard of my work, then? Why, Sarah..." His widow pointed her empty fork at their hostess in a teasing gesture. Daniel wasn't sure anyone but him caught the slight wavering in her arm before she retracted it. "You didn't tell me you'd shared about my mercantilian efforts."

Amazingly, she made it sound like *rep*tilian. And now instead of a phony-French doxy questioning his mistress-to-be, all Daniel saw across the table was a blowsy viper in fake rubies.

He set his fork down and leaned back in his chair, ready to be amused.

Sarah, he thought, masked her surprise plausibly well. Reaching for her wineglass, she took a delayed sip. Stalling? For herself or the friend she sought to shield? Returning the glass to the table, she met and held every gaze intent on the byplay. "Aye. But I could not resist. Forgive me. I know your wares are exclusive to Mr.—" A quick gloved hand made its way to Sarah's lips, as did a soft blush to her face. "Pardon me. His is a *very* select shop and promised anonymity to my dear friend if she would but consent to sell her work exclusively through him. I can offer no less." Sarah placed one finger to her lips and appraised the group at large. "May I have your assurance of secrecy?"

Several heads bobbed and the woman next to him choked off a snicker.

When she was again composed, and keeping her voice low, the widow leaned forward and addressed the rapt crowd. "I do thank everyone most sincerely. Now let us talk of topics we've not sworn to secrecy. Dominique," she spoke directly to the vixen in forged finery, "do tell us of what ever book you now enjoy. I so love literary recommendations from new acquaintances."

"I do not read." Dominique bristled, looking as though she had no clue how the topic had escaped her grasp and segued back to *her*. (Daniel wasn't sure he knew either but it had been great fun witnessing the little charade—for he had no doubt one had just been enacted.) "Not your English drivel."

"Don't read at all, I vow," his companion-soon-to-be-mistress whispered beneath her breath. Then brightly, to the table at large, "Of course you don't," and before Dominique could take umbrage—for no one seemed inclined to come to *her* defense, he noted—Mrs. Hurwell turned the focus yet again. "What of you, Sarah? Have you finished either of those two volumes you purchased at Hatchards last week?"

"Yes—what did you buy?" Harrison's beauty vaulted in with sincere interest. "I just completed Byron's *The Corsair* and found it easier to put down than his other works."

"Oh, did you?" Sarah said with a sly look at the woman seated between them. "Mrs. Hurwell practically fawns over Lord Byron. I could hardly *rip* the pages from her grasp the last time she beheld them."

"Perhaps so," his widow demurred, "but once they'd served their purpose I relinquished them easily enough..."

And so it went. Most of the table's occupants engaging in light, meaningless banter with the lovely Mrs. Hurwell chiming in as appropriate.

Daniel found himself more than pleased.

She answered promptly and with an undercurrent of wit not everyone circling the table seemed privy to. Her responses, while intelligent and entertaining—to him at least—were concise, he noted with no little degree of appreciation. Neither did she instigate conversation but only responded when posed a direct query.

Exquisite. Could he have asked for better?

. . .

LORD TREMAYNE'S admiring analysis and pleasure over Dorothea's lack of verbosity would have most certainly been mitigated had he but known how she battled the inner longing to turn to him and inquire fifty and one assorted things: Was he always this quiet? Did he truly like the glazed shoe leather on his plate? (He must, he'd downed it with nary a blink.) Which poets did he find particularly fascinating? And what in heaven's name was a munsons muffler?

The servants brought out another course, this one glazed duck—she thought. It was a bit difficult to tell as the poor bird was so raw it was practically still swimming. Foregoing the foul fowl altogether, Dorothea picked nimbly through the macaroni noodles—they seemed safe enough, if a trifle undercooked—and allowed herself to admit what she *really* wanted to ask: Why had Lord Tremayne neglected to shave his chin whiskers?

Was he growing out his beard or did he not care enough about meeting her to bother? And did he always smell so nice? (A curious combination of cloves and honeysuckle that made her want to forego the filling noodles and lick him instead. Shameful, she knew, but the urge was undeniable.) What did he do with his days? Did he want *her* for his mistress? Had he any inkling yet, one way or the other? How often might he visit? *Was he married?*

Heavens to Hertfordshire, but just thinking of

everything she wanted to ask him was enough to keep her mute. Well, her chaotic thoughts *and* Sarah's counsel: *Take your cue from him.*

So this was a man who wanted quiet? She shoved aside the pang of disappointment at not finding a boon companion in her first foray into the demimonde.

Then she fortified her resolve because *quiet* she could do; wedded to Mr. Hurwell, she'd lived in it long enough.

HOW SOON COULD THEY LEAVE? Blazing ballocks, but he'd guillotine Penry if he'd arranged some drawn-out shadow play as he'd done the last time Daniel consented to attend one of these asinine public affairs. That one had been years ago at Sarah's standard-strumpet townhouse, before his friend had invested more than common sense recommended in his high flyer's accommodations and purchased her this near mansion. Louise had been enamored with the salacious shadow play and once they'd returned to her lodgings, had wanted him to perform a strip behind a sheet, backlit by the fire, for her amusement (he'd sooner swim the Thames—*bound* in a sheet).

He cringed at the memory. Thank God she'd found another protector, some American captain more flush in his pockets than his crown office had swept her off to his ship. She'd sent round a perfumed note before they'd sailed to make sure

Daniel knew she wasn't pining for him. He grunted. Not hardly. Who would pine for that bird-witted bird of paradise—when Paradise of another kind waited in the chair beside him?

A good night's sleep after a good round of frisking! He'd sing if he could, bellow out his delight—

What? Yammer out the tune of your faults?

By damn, he'd nearly forgotten.

A stunned, strangled groan worked its way free of his throat.

When she looked at him directly, the very source of his amazed consternation, a puzzled expression on her face, Daniel realized he'd gone practically the entire meal without uttering a word.

Gad, he was an arse.

4

BIRD-WITTED AS A CUCKOO OR LUCKY AS A LARK?

A voice so thrilling ne'er was heard
In spring-time from the Cuckoo-bird...

William Wordsworth, "The Solitary Reaper"

IN THE DIMMEST part of the large drawing room, Dorothea pressed her back into the wall so hard she heard it snap (her back that is, not the wall).

Escaping to make use of the necessary directly after the sliced fruit course had seemed a good idea a quarter hour ago; rejoining the ribald social scene seemed anything but. Because once her eyes adjusted to the reduced lighting, over half the candles being extinguished, she beheld the most startling sight on a settee not ten feet away.

So much for the men savoring after-dinner port and the women idle gossip. Dorothea gulped and tried to merge her spine into the wall. Mayhap she could close her eyes and pretend to vanish—

"*H*e really laps *h*er like *h*e means it, don't 'e?" a spirited voice asked in a conspiratorial whisper.

Startled to realize her secluded spot had been discovered, Dorothea nevertheless smiled when she realized who'd joined her. She'd met Susan before dinner and if the young woman's pronunciation wasn't consistent, her friendliness and sincerity of manner were.

Glad for the company, Dorothea promptly answered the H-heavy high flyer. "That he does."

Goodness, but she sounded woefully out of breath. Not taking her eyes from the couple both she and her companion spoke of, Dorothea filled her lungs and tried again. "I say, do all er, um..." How did one properly describe that which was so improper? Blazes! She could practically hear the saliva-induced suction from here! "Ah...do all titled gentlemen nurse themselves with such vigor upon the bosom of their paramours?"

"Wot?" The young woman's attempt at elocution slipped yet again. "Oh, you mean are they all so game when they suck on diddeys?"

"Um-mm..." When he switched his attention to the neglected nipple on the other side, she saw it was the gentleman with the large laugh and even larger nose.

Dorothea averted her eyes from the scandalous sight. But as though the unfamiliar tingling in her newly awakened breasts controlled her vision more than her sense of modesty did, her head immediately swung back. "I don't know that I've ever seen"—*or considered, and certainly haven't experienced*—"how such an activity might be done for so long and with such painstaking effort and zeal," she whispered to her companion. "He's very thorough, isn't he?"

Susan sighed hard enough to ruffle several of the gentleman's protruding nose hairs.

While Dorothea swallowed both laughter and dismay, her new friend answered with more than a hint of wistfulness. "Aye, Donny's—oops, I mean Lord Donaldson." Susan leaned close to confide, "'E told me to only call *h*im that when we were naked. Well, *h*e's one of the best I ever *h*ad. That man likes nipples more than a dry scone craves bacon-grease gravy, an 'e can kiss on 'em for a long while before *h*e goes diving lower."

Another sigh made her fond recollections clear, though Dorothea wasn't quite clear on what "diving lower" meant.

She had an inkling, an incredible, too-shocking-to-be-accurate inkling but decided 'twas best to stay mum. No need to shock Susan with her ignorance—or herself with the improbable, impossible truth if *lower* did not mean one's umbilicus.

"'E don't like just bein' with the same woman over an' over, so 'e never keeps a mistress but 'e'll pay you well fer a night or two—and damn me if I ain't goin' and fer-*for*gettin*g* my proper speech with you,

Mrs. H. You're not as *h*oity-toity as some of them others."

Flattered, if surprised, Dorothea said, "Thank you. I'm the last one to put on airs. I'm rather new at the trade myself."

"I figured that out when Dominasty went after you at dinner. She's a real bitch, that one is."

Dorothea barely managed to stifle her gasp at the vulgar word she'd never heard another female utter—discourses on breeding dogs notwithstanding. Certainly, no one had ever said it knowingly in her presence before.

"She's a miserable rip to anyone she sees as a threat," Susan continued. "Don't pay her no, I mean, *any* mind. Crikey, but these things won't quit droopin'!" Susan bent over and hauled up her skirt, revealing an indecent amount of thigh—thanks to the drooping stocking.

Dorothea politely averted her eyes. Only to encounter several other indecent sights.

About the *only* decent thing remaining was the cluster of men congregating near the hallway and spilling into the opposite room. The more plentiful wall sconces that direction lit them clearly. Lord Tremayne was among their number and these gentlemen, unlike the others closer to her, remained vertical and clothed.

Sarah waved and caught Dorothea's attention. A quick lift of her brows inquired how Dorothea got on, a slight tilt of her head asked whether she needed immediate rescuing.

Feeling infinitely more at ease now that she and Susan were engaged (and she no longer held up the wall alone), also curious what else the young woman might impart about "Donny" or diddeys or any other formerly forbidden topic, Dorothea smiled encouragingly. *I'm all right*, she hoped her expression conveyed. *Betwattled to the gills but still breathing. Hostess away...*

After an understanding nod, Sarah headed toward the nearest servant to confer over something, leaving Dorothea where she was—which was swallowing her surprise over Susan's continued actions (really, she balked at a raised skirt, given what else currently went on?). "Those are the most lovely stockings," Dorothea told her honestly. "I don't believe I've ever seen that shade of lavender before."

Certainly not on stockings. Dorothea's feet fairly lit up at the prospect—would lavender stockings feel any different than ordinary ones? Hers, all two and a half remaining pair, were dingy beige—years ago, they'd started out white—and sporting more than a snag or two, she was shamed to admit.

Task finished, Susan straightened and fluffed her skirts. "Aren't they the most rum color? Lord Denten got them for me when—"

At a shout, Susan glanced up, then her eyes fairly sparkled. "I 'ate to run off but looks like Cecilia's found us two gents fer the night." She squeezed Dorothea's elbow. "Now stop wringin' your hands and no one'll know how bedeviled by the jitters you are."

"Be well and thank you." Dorothea's parting words were lost when Susan's friend tromped over and grabbed her arm to drag her toward the waiting men.

Alone. Again.

Well now. That had been a refreshing exchange.

But Dorothea was still of two minds: Was she excited about the imminent physical prospects facing her later tonight or dreading them? Did she want this evening to be over swiftly and the die cast, her fate sealed, or did she want the minutes to eclipse slowly, giving her time to make the right decision?

Were the growing tingles in her abdomen anticipation over what might come? Or was her stomach simply seizing in a cramp because she'd not consumed enough food today? Or perhaps because it protested its recent and disastrous dinner?

Bah. Watching women abandon all sense of decorum because they enjoyed—nay, *encouraged*—the roving touch of a man was proving enlightening. Even thrilling, if she were honest.

Dorothea wanted to be scandalized by their behavior—she *should* be scandalized. But a heretofore unrecognized part of her found the couples' actions arousing. She was enticed to stare, even as part of her was compelled to turn away. The conflicting urges confused her almost as much as the man she'd come to meet.

Her eyes sought out his form again, though in truth, she'd been acutely aware of him all night.

Wretched man! Lord Tremayne hadn't attempted to converse with her during dinner, not once! Neither before nor after he'd so thoughtfully, so unexpectedly, sliced through all her misconceptions about peers when he'd adroitly severed the tough mutton for her. But still—not a word!

Did that mean he wasn't interested?

She sincerely hoped not. For if she were to indulge in sexual congress with another man—if some nipple-licking lord was going to place his hands and lips on her—then she desperately hoped *he* would be the one. Unlike her late husband, who had, all things considered, been rather nondescript, Lord Tremayne commanded attention without effort. The very air about him seethed with a dangerous excitement that made her feel both on edge and eager for another tantalizing taste.

"Well? Will he do?" Handing her a goblet of ratafia, Sarah came up and asked the question in a quiet but urgent voice, looking at Lord Tremayne who stood slightly apart from the crowd surrounding Lord Penry.

Grateful for something to strangle with her wayward hands, Dorothea took the glass by the stem and downed half the contents before coming up for air. "Sarah, why ever did you not introduce us? I believe without that formality, Lord Tremayne did not feel at liberty to address me directly."

"Oh, please say he didn't harp on that!" Sarah laughed without malice and her gaze found Dorothea's. "I deliberately left that to him so as not to embarrass you. Until you and he come to an official arrangement, I doubted you wanted it announced to the world at large that we'd intentionally matched you. I believe he's acquainted, at least by sight, with most everyone else, so I thought that the best way to proceed."

"Of course. Thank you, then, for your consideration." Dorothea couldn't stop her eyes from seeking him out.

At the sight of his tall, broad form, at contemplating pressing hers along it once they were alone, a strange mew of longing filled her.

Quite the opposite of what she experienced when Big Nose gained an armful as Dominique landed on his lap—and his hand promptly disappeared under her skirts. (So much for ardent bosom worship; now he seemed intent on, indeed, diving *lower*, in every sense of the term.)

"What do they discuss so animatedly?" she asked Sarah when one of the other men rounded on Lord Penry and gesticulated as she imagined might a newly headless chicken.

"The recent riots," Sarah answered gravely. "They've caused much contention to erupt in Parliament, as members debate the corn regulations. Penry and a handful of others have brought petitions, signatures numbering in the tens of thousands, and have spoken against the Corn Bill as it stands, but their protests have gone mostly unheard. As public unrest has grown to such a violent state, he's rallying support, hoping to prevail."

Dorothea had heard mention of the riots that swept through the city days ago. Angry mobs protesting in the most violent way, attacking the homes of specific peers and members of both Houses. Hearing of the tumult the morning following was a far cry from watching those directly involved discuss the issue with such heat.

The House of Lords. The House of Commons. The king—or in the current clime, his rascally son. Powerful men whose decisions shaped, for good or ill, their country. Never before had Dorothea reason to consider what all went on, how a single conversation at a small dinner party might change the course of history. It brought home how far her station was from those present tonight.

A clock seller, a watchmaker. That's who she'd been wedded to. Someone who lived by the ticking turn of the big hand and demanded she do the same: up at five dings, breakfast at six dongs, open the store at eight chimes (or, when she wasn't swift enough to misalign something after he repaired it, annoying cuckoos), and so on...until bed twelve hours later when again those horrendous cuckoo birds sang (for by now, Mr. Hurwell would've fixed them). Only to do the cycle all over again the following day. To the *minute*. For in Mr. Hurwell's eyes, untimeliness was akin to thievery, murder, and idle chatter.

The only time things ever varied was when a nearby horse race was to be had, and Mr. Hurwell abandoned his me*tick-tick-tick*ulous dignity for the thrill of equestrian gambling.

She'd made the mistake, once, of teasing him about it—his fascination with clocks and all things that dinged, donged or gonged—early in their marriage. A simple comment which led to a setting down of monumental proportions and the severe admonishment that "Levity has no place in the life of a hard-working Englishman. Or his wife's." Bah.

She'd soon come to adore the races he closed the shop to attend, for those were the only days Dorothea enjoyed any freedom, didn't have to plan her every action according to her husband's methodical, ding-dong dictates.

Come to think on it, she hadn't seen Lord Tremayne consult his timepiece even once tonight. *And* he'd been sufficiently unmindful to arrive late. How wonderful was that?

But she was beginning to wonder if he'd ever deign to glance at her again.

Wretched, intriguing, wonderfully tardy man!

"They'll be a while, I'd wager," Sarah said. "Though I daresay Anna is bursting at the seams to visit." Sarah gestured toward the pretty blonde of middle years occupying one of the chairs farthest from the men. "She's increasing," Sarah explained sotto voce with a smile as they made their way toward her. "Or she'd be in the thick of the debate."

Dorothea didn't know what stunned her more—that a woman might dare argue politics with not just a man (which was shocking enough) but an entire group of them *or* that her pregnancy seemed a joyous thing. Wouldn't that mean an end to her protected situation?

With a light touch to Sarah's arm, Dorothea halted their progress. "Her benefactor—Lord Harrison. He isn't angered by her condition?"

"On the contrary. They're both delighted. She lost an unborn babe last year, and I gather Harry's ensuring she takes every chance to rest this time around. Now don't look so worried... This is a joyous thing—for them. For *yourself*, simply practice what I told you each time you have relations with Tremayne and your chances of conceiving will be drastically reduced."

They'd be *completely* reduced unless he approached her.

A circulating waiter came by for their empty glasses and after placing hers and the one she had to pry from Dorothea's fingers on the tray, Sarah started forward again. "They were *trying*, dearest. Both of them want this child."

A second later she was being entertained by the *enceinte* woman.

The next few minutes flew by in a startling blur of whispers and laughs, which did much to calm the quadrille-dancing butterflies fluttering about Dorothea's middle. Anna was a joy, as pleasant and welcoming as Sarah if more critical toward those she had no tolerance for.

Hearing her blast the absent Louise as a bubble-headed ninny who deserved the coarse American she'd sailed off with, thereby informing Dorothea the woman most recently in Lord Tremayne's bed wasn't someone she need fear crossing paths with, greatly eased her chest. Laughing so hard when Anna launched into a diatribe about Italian accommodations only made it hurt anew but in a wonderful way.

Finally the men's talks wound down, due in part she was sure, to the enticement of several bored strumpets who took to climbing all over a few of the stragglers. Lord Harrison soon drifted over to steal his woman away after thanking his hostess.

"Hold tight to this one," Sarah told Anna after Lord Harrison effusively complimented dinner. "The devilish twinkle in his eyes tells you when he's spouting clankers. But he's so very sincere about it, I cannot help but approve."

Once they were gone and several other couples (*and* a couple of trios) followed—and once Sarah excused herself to ask Big Nose and Dominique to hie themselves off before soiling her settee—Sarah and Dorothea stood near where she'd begun the evening—the darkened corner, surveying Lord Tremayne and Lord Penry. Though the other men had drifted away, the gangly youth had joined them at some point. They were the only three still in earnest conversation.

"He's rather a magnificent specimen, is he not?" Sarah was staring straight at Lord Tremayne, leaving Dorothea in no doubt of whom she spoke. "And the way he fills out his inexpressibles..." Sarah made a sound of appreciation. "Impressive, to say the least."

Dorothea floundered. She wasn't used to discussing men or their attributes in detail.

Her murmur was noncommittal; her blush was not.

Sarah laughed quietly. "Don't mind me. Penry keeps me more than satisfied, financially and physically. I wouldn't be human, though, if I hadn't given a thought to being with Tremayne. Men like that don't seek to feather their love nest every day, which is why I've championed for the two of you to meet. Tragically, it so often seems the attractive ones are either insanely boring or horribly depraved."

"Depraved? You mean wicked? Lord Tremayne?"

Now why did that thought not have *her* hieing off? Mayhap, after years of restrained living, she craved a little wickedness—along with lateness—in her life.

"Certainly not. At least, not that I'm aware of. Tremayne keeps to himself more than most, but I've always found him sincere. A bit rough around the edges at times but charming nevertheless. Penry speaks highly of him. And the entire time I've been with Penry, Tremayne has only had the one mistress. Does that not bode well for your extended future?"

Rather than contemplate the future, Dorothea voiced her present concern. "I'm not sure he's interested in me. He hasn't said much." That was an understatement.

"Oh, posh. Have you not noticed the way he's devoured you with his gaze on multiple occasions?"

She hadn't. With a slight shake of her head, Dorothea commented, "He is very handsome in a ruggedly appealing way." Another understatement —and when had she begun to think of him thus? A powerfully built hulk of a man who towered over her by nearly a foot and had thick, coffee-colored hair—and whiskers—along with a propensity for sparse conversation...

How could she find that attractive? But then her nostrils flared and her mouth watered at the memory of his divine scent as though her other senses overrode that of sight. Aye. She found him easy on the eye, *if* easily intimidating.

But initial impressions were often erroneous. After all, hadn't she found Mr. Hurwell pleasant and agreeable during their first few meetings? Enough, certainly, to countenance a marriage to the man when her father pushed to secure her future.

Perhaps time with Lord Tremayne might soften his harsh edges (and ultimately find a razor blade scraping those whiskers to perdition).

Was she as bird-witted as her former husband's stupid cuckoo clocks? For beginning to yearn for a man she knew nothing about? Or could Sarah's earlier claim possibly be correct—was she fortunate enough to have found the answer to her unspoken prayers?

"Can you do this, do you think? Be intimate with him?" Sarah asked intently. "It's not too late to call a halt, but I truly believe he's a gentleman in every sense. He isn't addicted to drink nor to gambling. Doesn't overindulge at the table and isn't a pinch farthing when it comes to the ready—he kept Louise dressed in style and she always had pin money to fritter." Sarah gave an indulgent snort. "From what I can tell, his worst vice is his propensity toward tardiness, a minor inconvenience at best."

Now that she'd seen him, been intrigued by his manner and enticed by his scent, something akin to panic squeezed her chest at the thought of *not* going through with her intended plans for the evening.

"Aye! I want to go home with him tonight." Good heavens. She sounded overly excited about the prospect. This was supposed to be something she *had* to do, not something she *wanted* to do. Dorothea tempered her tone. "Well, if I absolutely *must* have a protector, then I believe Lord Tremayne will do."

Quite nicely.

"If you're sure?"

Why was Sarah expressing doubts now? It had been her idea to begin with! Dorothea might have been brought up to never remotely consider such an arrangement, but she also knew hunger. The newly added lace at her cuffs reminded her she also knew fear.

After finally meeting a titled gentleman in want of a mistress, one who took pains to considerately make mincemeat of her mutton, was she sure? She was positive that being with him far surpassed any other alternatives open to her at present.

"I am," Dorothea said with an emphatic nod, guilty excitement tingling in her belly. "But does he not need to approach me?" And before the clock struck midnight? She'd been acutely aware of the eleven resonant bells a while ago, chiming out her doom if he didn't get on with it.

"Fie! More often than not, men must be shown what they need. Are you game?"

Before Dorothea could nod her assent, Sarah grabbed her hand and was resolutely tugging her in the direction of the three men.

A short while earlier...

"Who's the runt?" Daniel nodded toward the lanky kid grinning at him from a distance. It was a touch eerie—the cub didn't appear to be gawking at anyone else.

Now that Penry had spoken his piece and Harry echoed the points with convincing—and enviable—ease, and between them they'd managed to sway at least three of the others to give their cause due consideration, it was past time to secure his little widow.

But something about the way the kid had been staring at him all evening set off alarm bells. Like the ticking of an overloud clock one couldn't ignore, Daniel had the feeling an explosion was about to detonate.

A feeling he shrugged off—why borrow trouble that didn't exist?

"That's Everson's youngest." Penry waved the cub over. "He's a huge admirer but you need—"

"Admirer of what? Loose women?"

"Tell me I didn't just hear that." Penry shot him a dark look. "You're under duress else I wouldn't let that slide without a slap."

A slap? As in challenge him to a duel? Over a jest? A quip barely slighting the man's mistress? When had Penry become so protective? And what was he nattering on about now?

"...to meet you." Penry spoke so low, Daniel saw his lips move more than heard him. "Fair warning, though, he—" Penry broke off when the boy raced the last few steps and reached them in a blink. "Tremayne, this eager fellow here is Thomas Everson, Jim's youngest. But he prefers to go by Tom," Penry said with the ease of long acquaintance.

With not more than a score of years under his belt—if that—the young buck stood taller than either of them, six-four or better, and his lack of muscle made him appear as long and thready as a weed. He had a shock of red hair and the type of fair skin that blushed abominably. Young Tom also had a smile wider than Penry's slab of a dining table.

"Tom, as you already know, this here is Daniel Holbrook, the Marquis of Tremayne."

Daniel gave a slight bow to acknowledge the introduction. Very slight—he wasn't used to looking up to anyone. Not since reaching his majority and the height of six-three, not since escaping the estate and his brute of a father.

Tom didn't look anything like *his* sire. Everson was a stout, beefy fellow well into his fifties. Without a daughter to his name, he was known more for his brood of nine sons than his talent in the ring, but Daniel had always found him a jovial, good-natured companion when they sparred. One who'd bluster on about anything with a smile on his face—even when Daniel's fist had just connected with it.

Everson was often accompanied by a son or two, but Daniel didn't remember ever seeing this one. Tom beamed at him and thrust his hand out in a casual show of greeting not found among mere acquaintances, never found from a pup to a peer.

Startled by the gesture as much as surprised to find himself grinning back, Daniel clasped Tom's outstretched hand. But holding on to the smile almost killed him when the boy started to speak.

"Muh-muh-muh-mmmmu-mmmmmm-ister Hollllllllbrook, sssssssir," Tom forced out Daniel's seldom-heard surname while holding his gaze, the boy's own expression as guileless as could be.

Kaboom! The bomb went off. Pieces of shrapnel, of syllables, exploding around him.

"*Ahmpa.*" The nonsense syllable blasted through the debris. "Mmmmmeannnnn Llllllord-lord T-t-t-t-tr-trey-*mayne*!"

Was this a joke? A cruel jest? Penry getting in a dig after that thoughtless loose-woman crack? But no, Tom continued his laborious speech—and his clutching of Daniel's hand—with both enthusiasm and unbridled excitement.

"I've ad-mmmmred you *ahmp* sin-sin-since that-that-that-that match in Do-Dover."

And Penry, when Daniel shot a panicked glance his direction, only looked apologetic. His expression screamed a guilty *I tried to tell you*.

Realizing there was no help from that quarter, Daniel felt his head fight against him, his neck muscles objecting when he forced them back, returning his gaze to the boy's. Who was still smiling, still exuberantly massacring everything he uttered. Still gripping Daniel's hand.

"Ffffffellled Thomp-*ah*-son fas-fas-faster than lightning, you did." A garbled breath, a few unintelligible sounds, then, "'Twas a beaut, my lord, a beaut of-fa-fa a fight, it was. Made me pa-pa-pa-*roud* to see it-t-t-t!"

Daniel was exhausted. Simply listening, without cringing, required so much strength. He didn't know how much longer he could hold himself together. Every muscle screamed in protest, bunched tight from his ankles to his armpits.

But the kid wasn't finished—with his speech or with pumping Daniel's arm. "Yessirreee, ever since that-that-that-jab-you-you-lan-lan-landed in the fourth round, I've been affffffff-ter Papapapa to 'duce me..."

Tom went on, haltingly at times, furiously fast at others but always exuberantly, putting to shame the agony Daniel experienced each time he even thought to open his mouth.

He endured more accolades than he deserved, more praise than he warranted, but through the remainder of the painful recitation, the inarticulate articulations, he never tried to retrieve his hand and he never—not once—allowed his gaze to falter from the young man's.

It was excruciating.

As though he watched a mirror image of himself—though one nearly half his age who truly had things worse off than he did. A reflection that hurt, not so much because looking at it made him uncomfortable—which admittedly, it did—but because seeing *this* side of it, seeing how *his* image could have been projected into the world had he possessed a father like Everson, someone encouraging instead of cutting, someone constructive instead of destructive, made Daniel long for what he'd never had. Never *have.*

A different father and older brother. A different childhood. Acceptance, tolerance, lack of self-consciousness.

It made him long for a different life. A past not punctured with doubt and shame. A future not burdened with the expectation of failure.

It made him long to be anywhere but here.

Tom's speech was riddled and rutted with so many stops, starts and stumbles, it was a wonder he still stood. Still garbled out admiration that only scraped Daniel raw.

Finally, after his jaw had already started cramping in sympathy, the boy wound down. And just then noticed he still maintained possession of Daniel's hand.

"Oh-oh-oh-suh-suh-suh-*suhrry*, so sorry!" Tom's grip had tightened during his monologue and Daniel suspected it had been totally involuntary. Holding on to a lifeline so he didn't drown. One he now dropped like a hot coal. "Geh-geh-geh-geh-*g*et-t-t-t 'cited and for-g-g-get-t-t."

And still the kid was smiling.

Deuced amazing.

Damned impressive.

How was he still going? Daniel couldn't fathom it. Tom had to be exhausted, the lack of air caused from all the muscles in his mouth and larynx seizing up on him, freezing out his breath, starving his body...

But dammit, he kept charging forward.

"Seen you at other b-b-b-b-bouts-bouts, I have-have-hav*eh*. Never miss one if-if-if-fff-I-can-help-help-help-*ah*-it but that one's mmmmmmmmmy-my-my fav'rite!" He glanced at Daniel's hand and his cheeks flushed crimson. "Ap-p-ologize, I do! *Ackpm.* For-got-got-got myself."

Giving his mangled fingers a ginger stretch, Daniel raised his beleaguered hand to the boy's shoulder when Tom paused for a breath.

He gave a gentle squeeze. *Forgiven. Nothing to forgive, in fact,* he wanted to say. But he couldn't. Not after witnessing—after *living*—Tom's butchered speech.

So he nodded. And thought fast. But talked slow. "Honored." Daniel brought his hand back to his side and felt strangely bereft. "High...praise you..."

Deliver? Bestow? Dammit! What else? *Think, man, think. Don't start mumbling like an idiot!*

5

PAST VS PRESENT VS PASSION

"Father, father, where are you going?
O do not walk so fast!
Speak, father, speak to your little boy,
Or else I shall be lost."

The night was dark, no father was there,
The child was wet with dew;
The mire was deep, and the child did weep,
And away the vapour flew.

William Blake, "The Little Boy Lost"

DON'T BE AN IDIOT!

Oh, God. Memories swamped him, made his ears ring. Strangled his tongue.

How many times had he heard that in his youth? *Don't mutter like a dolt! Stop yammering like a fool!*

Only idiots can't speak their mind. Guess that makes you an idiot, then, don't it? Get out of here, idiot-boy, can't stand the sight of you!

It hit him like a lightning bolt. One that flashed fierce and hard, sizzled through his veins as though his blood had caught fire. Not once had he thought of young Everson as an idiot. As something to belittle. Not once!

But himself? At the mere possibility of tripping over a letter or two, Daniel started thinking like his father. Condemning and cruel.

Nausea roiled through his gut as the force of his memories outweighed the knot of dinner by a stone.

And Tom Everson was still waiting. Penry still watching his every move like a mother hen protecting chicks from a fox.

"High p-praise— *Arghem.*" He cleared his throat to mask the fumble. As though he swallowed metal spikes with every sound, it felt scratched raw. "You shower on me," he somehow managed to say without mangling. Without running for the carriage as though Death chomped at his heels. "High... praise...in...deed."

When would he ever be rid of the old man's legacy? When, goddammit?

Peripherally he caught sight of Sarah and Mrs. Hurwell, heads together in conversation, eyes darting his direction. By damn! He'd forgotten all about her. His new mistress.

If he hadn't blundered that beyond salvaging. Ignore her during dinner. Neglect her afterward. Go home empty-handed and mistressless. Listless. Lonely.

Again.

But he couldn't abandon the boy, not even if it meant missing out on the pretty widow. Not after the courage the kid had just displayed. Was still showing, in fact.

"Wellllll deserved, mmmmy-my-my lord, well de-deserved! Muh-muh-muh-*ight* you work with me, Lllllllllord Tremayne? In-in-in-the-the-ring?"

Only a heartless bastard would turn the boy down. Would be so cruel.

"Will-will-will you t-t-t-t-*teach* me?"

"Absolutely not."

And don't look at me like that. I can't be around you and be reminded.

Of what I never had.

That I'm turning into him.

Devil take me! I'm turning into him—the man I loathe most in all the world. I'm sitting like him, thinking like him, acting *like him.*

Fire burned along his lip, the old scar reminding him he'd never be free.

But he had to say something else. Couldn't leave it at that. Couldn't bear the dimming of the eager features, hated seeing the excitement falter into embarrassment, the hero-worship turning to hurt.

'Tis nothing to do with you, Daniel wanted to shout at Tom. But in truth it had everything to do with him.

Daniel couldn't be around Tom Everson and not

constantly remember, not forever compare. He couldn't interact with the boy without seeing the life he *could've* had, had his father not been such a loathsome monster.

Daniel fought the constriction in his throat to force out, "Not just you...boy. I...don't...train." Mayhap not, but he did sound like a hard arse. "New fighters. Only spar with ...those ex...p'renced." He'd left off a syllable or two but couldn't bring himself to care. He only wanted to escape.

By damn, his insides had been dipped in burning coals, his whole body overly warm in places, searing hot in others. His neck burned, blistered by the fear. He had to get away before the rest of him turned to ash.

A light, joyful laugh drew his reluctant gaze across the room. Mrs. Hurwell, flushed from wine and he knew not what else, looked more fetching than ever. She caught his glance and gave him an encouraging, if timid, smile.

His fiery gut clenched with the renewed thrum of desire. Oblivion—for a few moments at least. That's what time with her body promised.

But he couldn't stomach *talking* to her for God's sake, not now. Not for the amount of time required to do the pretty before he plunged inside her to pound away his past.

Damn. He balled his sore hand at his side, contemplating: the woman or his sanity?

Who needed a new mistress? His bruised fingers should be sufficient for the task. If he yanked his pipe long enough, maybe he could jerk the growing pain right out the tip along with his spunk.

"Tremayne." At the unmistakable warning from Penry, Daniel wrenched his gaze back to Tom.

The kid was blinking fast, trying to hide the hurt. He didn't quite succeed. The smile he flashed was as wide as ever, but it didn't come close to reaching his eyes. "I-I-I-I-I unnnnnnnnn-der-der-sta-sta-sta-stand," he spoke softer and without any inflection. "Should've known beh-beh-beh-ter-ter-ter. *Mmmm-mmnnnnnnn. Ap. Ap. Mmmmnnnn.*"

Daniel missed the eagerness that'd characterized Tom's earlier efforts. But God help him, he couldn't miss how Tom's elocution had faltered, grown worse, less comprehensible. Leading him to believe the boy now shuffling back and forth on his feet had practiced the lines beforehand, rehearsed what he'd come to say.

But never thought to rehearse a rejection.

"Un-un-understandstandstand, I d-d-d-do. Papa told me not-not to pester you-you-yyyyyyyyyou. Should havvvvvvvvv-*eh-eh* listennnnnned. *Mmmmmm...*"

When the word refused to come despite several seconds' effort, when his lips persisted in staying glued together despite his obvious efforts to pry them apart, Tom jerked his head to the side and reached up to slap his face, a hard *thwack* Daniel felt slam across *his* mouth. The slash of a cane instead of a palm. He bit the inside of his cheek to keep from crying out.

Tom looked back at Daniel, unshed tears welling in his eyes. The sight punched him in the stomach harder than any blow he'd ever received. "F-fa-fault. Meh-meh-meh-*mine*."

Daniel wanted to take the rejection back. Wanted to offer to meet the brave young man next week. To teach him everything he could.

He wanted to offer to be his friend.

But he did none of those things. Throat tight, neck aching with the strain, teeth and tongue trembling, he fisted his throbbing fingers tighter and inclined his head in a curt show of acknowledgment or dismissal—he knew not which, and he wasn't about to linger long enough to figure it out.

Before he could stop himself, Daniel pushed past Penry and stepped around Tom.

"Tremayne!" Penry called him back. But he kept moving forward, blindly racing for a way out.

You'll burn in hell, Satan spawn, his sire had screamed at him once (more than once if he were honest). He very well might burn, Daniel knew. But it wouldn't be for the sins his father falsely attributed to him. It would be for running away and crushing a young man's spirit. For sacrificing another man's dreams to preserve his own delusions of manhood.

In seconds, he reached the main door and waited impatiently while the grim-faced butler retrieved his coat and other paraphernalia. The moment it was within reach, Daniel coiled his fingers tight around the shaft of his fancy walking stick, as though only it could keep him from drowning in the quicksand the night had become. His elaborate walking stick—a useless item, but Elizabeth had given it to him years ago, claiming she'd blessed it with all manner of herbs and enchantments, and he'd brought it tonight for luck.

For luck. What a laugh.

He transferred the cane so he could shrug into his coat, his damn hand missing the armhole on the first two attempts, no matter that the butler held it out for him.

"Lord Tremayne!" The feminine voice bit through the haze of guilt prodding his frantic actions. "Are you off so soon? And...and *alone*?"

Wrenching the coat from the butler, he shoved it over his arm and gripped the walking stick. Smoothing his hand over the cool ivory ball at the top, seeking a measure of composure anywhere he might find it, he turned to face the obstacle. For now, all he wanted was *gone*. Gone from this place. Gone from his damnable memories.

Sarah and Mrs. Hurwell.

It took a second to register that it was the widow who'd called out to him, who gazed at him inquiringly, no doubt seeking understanding.

Daniel opened his mouth to send her on her way, to say he'd changed his mind. But with one good look at her, he snapped it shut.

Because instead of accusing condemnation, as her friend's expression held, the widow's countenance reflected a remnant of the wounded look he'd just caused on Tom Everson's face. Instead of angry, she looked baffled, disconcerted by his inexplicable retreat.

Hell. He was disconcerted by the whole damn evening.

Being this close to her again only brought home how much. He was attracted to her, of that there was no doubt. He wanted to know—nay, *feel*—what she could do with her mouth. So easily could he imagine how heavenly it would be to banish the hell brimming in his mind by hammering into her soft and welcoming body. "Ah, the lovely Mrs. Hurwell..."

Well, that came out flawlessly. Maybe *she*, rather than his ivory-handled walking stick, would prove to be his good-luck charm. "I am d-delighted...to mmake your acquain...tance."

And maybe she wasn't.

Blast it! The scene with the cub had definitely addled his mouth.

Fortunately, some sauced fancy piece—half her bosom modestly covered, the other half bouncing with abandon—chose that moment to run by, an indiscreet lordling hot on her heels. Her squeals and his shouts camouflaged Daniel's massacred greeting. Any other time the vulgar display might have made him frown; tonight he was hard pressed not to blow the trollop a kiss.

He turned back to the widow. As though the bawdy exhibit of bare breast had never been flaunted, she stared at him with calm, pale eyes the color of the underside of a velvet leaf. Beautiful eyes, oddly haunting, threatening to drown him in curiosity and uncertainty.

If any decency resided in him at all, he'd pay her for the month and give her to Tom Everson. Salvage his pride with the gesture.

But he was too damn selfish.

Mrs. Hurwell had come here for him. Dammit, she was meant to be *his*.

He knew he'd disappointed her, taking off the way he had. Yet still she gazed at him with something akin to hope. The wary stance she employed, the perceptible, if squashed, optimism—as though poised to run herself but reluctant to do so—put him in mind of Cyclops when he'd rescued the dog. She might put on a brave front, but he couldn't shake the notion she was quaking inside.

It only endeared her to him.

Though Sarah hovered right behind her, a fierce frown pinching their hostess's forehead, it was the widow who commanded his attention. She had a way about her that drew him mightily. A pliableness to her features, a soft hesitancy to her eyes as she stood there after chasing him down as he tried to escape his past...

By damn, he might not be as brave as Tom Everson, but he was man enough to speak up for what he wanted—which was her in his bed. Posthaste.

"Shall we depart?" The smooth delivery put him on his guard; he didn't trust his mouth to be so cooperative again.

Damn, his neck ached abominably. He just

wanted to prig her and go to sleep. In her arms if she'd let him.

Hoping to alleviate the growing tension climbing up his jaw, he stretched his neck under the guise of transferring his walking stick to his opposite hand. He proffered her his free arm, the one unburdened by his haphazardly folded coat. "I"—*desire you fiendishly*—"wish to be off and would prefer we... go...to...gether."

When she hesitated, her gaze darting between him and her friend, Daniel intentionally relaxed his jaw, softened his posture. If he was scowling at her as he feared, she'd be a noddy to go anywhere with him.

As casually as he could manage, he lowered his arm. "'Tis your choice of course...but I would...be honored should you..." *Decide?* Nay! He quickly cast about and finished in a rush, "Choose-accompany-me."

Giving her a moment, trying not to berate his brain for panicking, he ordered his heart rate to slow. Deliberately, with every appearance of one with idle time on their hands, he strolled past her and approached Sarah to make his bow.

"Mm..." *Miss? Mrs.?* Blazing ballocks, he had no clue what her last name was, *Penry's woman* being how he typically thought of her—*if* he thought of her at all.

Wholly aware of the woman staring at his backside, the woman likely debating whether she wanted to see it bedside, he took a desperate breath and prayed his mouth wouldn't seize up. He started anew. "Sarah. Thank you for including me...tonight. Most gracious of..." Hell, he was growing hoarse. A hoard of frogs having jumped in his mouth along with his foot. "Of you."

He heard the widow shift in place and angled his head, silently watched the byplay between the women. Sarah's brows rose inquiringly and Mrs. Hurwell gave a slight nod, then stepped forth, ready to accompany him.

But then Penry's woman stood on tiptoes, pressing on his shoulder until he tilted his head, whereupon she whispered something to him that had *his* brows shooting skyward.

And the scowl returning full force to his face.

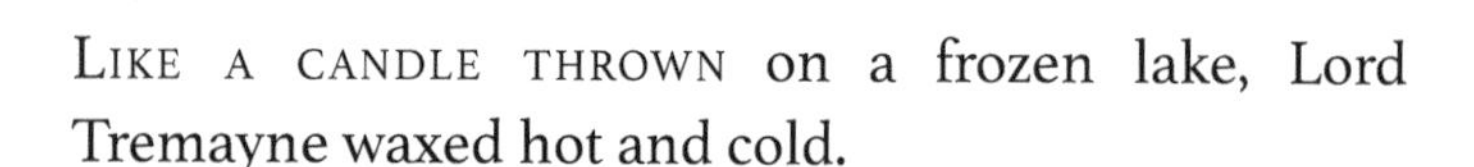

LIKE A CANDLE THROWN on a frozen lake, Lord Tremayne waxed hot and cold.

When he swung back to face her, his frown once again in place, Dorothea feared this time the downward tilt was etched in stone.

What had Sarah just said to cause its return?

She faltered as she reached him, her already shaky confidence wavering at the unholy glower he leveled her way. Fierce, then fiercer still, yet she couldn't bring herself to walk away. Or to truly want to.

Because in the brighter entryway, the bruises hiding beneath his whiskers were unmistakable.

And despite the hint of a scar on his lip, despite his formidable presence and fearsome grimace, she instantly felt an accord with him.

Had she not sewn lace on her cuffs for the very same reason? To mask unsightly bruises—though she doubted *his* were from a grubby, grabby landlord.

Suspecting the reason for his facial scruff lessened her dislike of it.

On the surface, she worried whether Sarah had landed her with a ruffian, a man inclined to shows of temper. But deeper, almost instinctually, her mind contradicted that assumption: Would a ruffian slice her serving? Would a royster have so many of his peers jockeying to greet him upon his arrival? Or monopolizing his attention after dinner?

Admittedly, Lord Tremayne possessed a most distinguished countenance, when one troubled themselves to look beneath the angry façade. The side whiskers in front of his ears and angling toward his jaw were shaped most adroitly, tempting her fingers to smooth along their contours, to seek out that tiny indentation bisecting both lips on a slant.

His posture was exquisite, the breadth of his chest impressive. His deep, somewhat gravelly voice, when he chose to bestow it, reverberated through her in the most invigorating way. And really, given the placid years that stretched behind her, was she not due some invigoration?

Dorothea shifted in place, considering.

If she wasn't meant to be with him, would she still

feel so inexplicably jealous upon seeing where his gaze had landed mere seconds ago—on the voluptuously exposed breast of the circling cuckoo in their midst?

Regardless! Dorothea chose not to evaluate how her own less-than-charming charms compared in the size-and-bounce arena.

She'd counter his every frown with a smile as long as his actions didn't pose a threat. But lay one finger on her in anger and she'd take a boot to his crown office, then one to Sarah's posterior for placing her in jeopardy.

That image fortifying her, Dorothea smiled past her nerves and allowed her reckless enthusiasm to show. "Lord Tremayne, I would very much like to accompany you, if that is still your wish."

His expression inscrutable, he grasped her gloved hand and pulled her forward as he bent to place a kiss just above the bend of her wrist.

"Mistress Hurwell?" his deep voice intoned as he looked past the length of her arm and sought her gaze. "My wishes have not changed."

This close to him again, with his big, strong hand holding gently to her fingers, the warmth from his breath reaching through the leather, her arm practically melted. "Call me Dorothea, please."

His grimace tightened perceptibly.

What? Had she crossed some line? Her fingers flexed within his.

He immediately unclenched his jaw and swallowed. Giving his head an abrupt shake, he stroked his thumb over her trembling fingers. "Thea, I think. It suits you...better."

Who was she to argue? At the heated look in his amber eyes, she feared she would've agreed if he'd suggested her new name be "Turtle".

Sarah stood a short distance away, foot tapping on the floor, arms crossed, eyebrow raised, waiting for more—from both of them, Dorothea sensed.

She looked back at Lord Tremayne (looked *up*, more precisely, given how he'd straightened). Her smile came naturally this time. "Thea. Would be lovely to hear it again," she told him. "'Tis what my mum called me when I was a girl."

"Are you agreeable?" Lord Tremayne cleared his throat and his gaze drifted to where he maintained possession of her hand. "Ah...to our union?"

Her palms were sweating in her gloves. She longed to rip them off and touch—

Places she likely shouldn't.

Was she agreeable? Goodness, he'd already seduced her entire arm; she was eager for him to seduce the rest of her.

"Aye." Her head jerked in a nod. "Quite."

As *Thea* (how appropriate—a new name to go with her new life) closed the distance between them, Sarah gave her a relieved nod and glided away. Now it was just her and her new protector—and the hovering butler, his eyes painstakingly averted, her reticule dangling off one finger.

Lord Tremayne saw it as well and released her.

While he put on his greatcoat, Thea reached for the small purse. “Thank you, Simms.”

Free of the feminine burden, Simms nodded toward a footman who opened the large door. A blast of icy spray swirled inside, nipping her feet with the threat of frost. Dorothea stamped them in place. “I am ready, my lord.”

“Your cloak?” Lord Tremayne sounded incredulous at the lack.

Her “cloak”—the coat of Mr. Hurwell’s she’d taken to wearing after his demise, being both warm and worn, thereby easily overlooked in the stews.

Rather than admit she’d chosen not to wear the tattered rag—one sleeve ripped completely off thanks to the most recent tussle with Grimmett—she pretended she hadn’t heard his question. Winding the strings of her reticule through the fingers he’d so recently caressed, she queried, “I’m to accompany you home, then?”

“I’ve arranged for your lodgings.” He stilled the nervous gesture by placing her arm on his. Her eyes swept from the sight of the new cream-colored gloves—thank you, Sarah!—atop his muscular forearm covered in dark wool, up to his face.

“We could retire there now?” His lips quirked in what she suspected was meant to be a reassuring smile.

Reassuring to a tart in truth, perhaps.

Thea swallowed her apprehension. “I would like nothing better, my lord,” she said rather convincingly, she hoped. “Lead on.”

Which he did, the large man with the intimidating scruff and inviting scent escorting her out of the safety of Sarah's home and into the dark, damp unknown.

With nary another word.

IN MOMENTS they were ensconced in his magnificent carriage, a grand conveyance far surpassing any other coach or hack she'd ever climbed into. The night air was thick from the day's rains, the cobblestones slick, but as the horses pranced forward and the well-oiled wheels turned smoothly, Thea couldn't help but marvel how she was—wonder of wonders—snug and safe.

If at sixes and sevens over how to go on from here. Lord Tremayne remained stubbornly mute and she claimed not the courage nor the fortitude to break the silence.

In such close confines, his alluring scent was stronger. Or perhaps she still reacted to the lung-expanding whiff she'd stolen when he handed her up and had seen her comfortably seated on the plush bench before settling his large frame into the one across from her.

Four feet, mayhap five. 'Twas all that separated their upper bodies. But it seemed a mile.

A single lamp lit the interior. Lit one side of his harsh face and the ivory knob of the walking stick his leather-encased thumb methodically stroked.

Lit her lap where she twined and tangled her

fingers as she battled two horribly opposed notions: her gloves or the door?

Her gloves, she was sorely tempted to rip off so she might touch his whiskers, could learn whether they were prickly as she suspected, or possibly, absurdly, soft to the touch. A most contrary yearning, given how she also contemplated opening the coach door and hurling herself into the night, fleeing the intensity of his presence...

Wholly aware of his speculative gaze evaluating her person, Thea was riddled with self-doubt now that they were alone. It was nearly time to lie in the bed she'd recklessly made.

The bed he'd bought, as surely as he'd bought her favors.

Uncertainty besieged her. She lifted back the curtain and focused on what she knew lay beyond the security of his richly appointed carriage: Grimmett, hunger...and unsavory mounds of mice doodles.

In the meager light afforded by the dwindling lantern, Daniel studied the subdued Widow Hurwell. *Thea.*

Seemingly immune to the frigid air, she sat with her back straight against the squabs. Both feet, encased in scuffed leather slippers, were placed firmly on the floor and her hands were knotted in her lap.

If he didn't know better, he'd think she was on her way to her execution, not her new home.

Did she seek to avoid him? Or was she simply interested in their destination? With rapt fascination, she gazed out toward the darkened streets, tilting her head to survey both where they headed and where they'd been.

The action exposed the pale skin of her cheek and throat.

A throat sans woolen scarf. A body—now trembling—attired in anything but a fashionable state.

"Your...belongings?" he asked. Other than the small reticule hanging from her wrist, she didn't have any personal effects. *No cloak?* No cape, nor pelisse? *Nothing?* He was still baffling over that discovery.

A slight movement of her head indicated she heard his question although it was a moment before she answered. "I'll retrieve my things tomorrow."

He thought to offer assistance, but she continued before he could phrase the words. "There isn't much, really. Only a few articles of clothing." She glanced at him and added, "Nothing I'd miss if everything vanished during the interim." A shy smile, then she returned to contemplating the view beyond the carriage. And he returned to contemplating her skin.

Delicate, smooth, inviting... Inviting his touch, his lips?

Sarah's parting words rose up to haunt him. *Mind you moderate your passions with her, Tremayne. Don't rush your fences and let your ardor overwhelm her.*

What the devil had Penry's woman meant by that caution? The one she'd whispered frantically in his ear just before they'd left.

Moderate his passions? Talk about interfering with his plans for the night.

He shifted in his seat and Thea jumped.

She turned from the window, letting the curtain fall back, and fixed her gaze on him. Her large, surprisingly pale eyes met his in the feeble lantern glow—the fuel needed refilling. But he was glad for it. Some of the starch seemed to go out of her spine the more the flame flickered.

He was acutely aware how his arousal increased as her steady regard lengthened.

Those eyes of hers did things to him. A soft jade green, her gaze held his without wavering. He'd only seen that exact shade once before, during a trip to the coast when he was a boy and his family still intact.

He and David had loved splashing in the ocean, watching the waves break upon the mossy, rock-crested shore.

She blinked, her expression unchanging, and Daniel shook himself.

Gad. He hadn't thought of that time in years. Robert had been off at school. He and David barely seven and, as always, inseparable; Ellie but a babe trailing after them. It was so clear he could taste the salt coming off the ocean, feel the chill of the water, the roughness of the rocks as he and his twin competed in a crab-catching contest, Mama laughing at their antics while Father indulgently looked on. That was before their sire had become such a beast.

The memory threatened to turn him maudlin and Daniel blamed her—Thea, with the moss-colored eyes. The refined features. The full lips.

Blasted ballocks—temper his passions? When all he wanted was to banish that lace fichu out the window and plunder her mouth with his while he plunged his hand down her dress to plunder the rest of her?

So he could fondle a handful of pointy-tipped breast and stop thinking of mossy banks, ocean discoveries and *moderating* his bloody passions.

His well-sprung carriage gave an uncharacteristic lurch as his driver hollered at another.

Instinctively Daniel's arm shot out to steady Thea but 'twas unnecessary. She'd done no more than bobble in place, as though staring at him silently, unnervingly, somehow gave her inner strength.

Disconcerting, it was. Desirable too. Deuce—

Another sharp swerve cut off the thought.

"Sorry, milord!" Roskins called out. "All's right now, it is!"

To acknowledge the apology, Daniel tapped the head of his walking stick on the roof twice, then replaced it beside him, all without ever taking his eyes from hers.

And still she watched him watching her.

The constant *clippety-clop* of the horses filled the

gently swaying carriage. That and the sound of his and Thea's breathing. Gad, she was quiet. Louise would have blathered on enough to wear out his wattles.

He reached up to rub one, just to make sure his hearing was still intact.

How many times had he been grateful there was no void for him to fill? Conversely, how many times had he wished for a latch upon the hinges of her jaw so he could stop the incessant chatter?

He'd tolerated the tavern-grade soliloquies on bonnets and baubles and butterflies, pleased naught was required of him in response. Yet he'd yearned for silence on occasion, to be blessed with a modicum of restful, peace-filled companionship.

Did he not have his wish now? Silence.

Peaceful, horrible, grating silence.

One that threatened to allow the guilt from earlier to swell and—

No. None of that now. He wouldn't think of Tom Everson or how he'd treated the boy. Wouldn't remember the crestfallen look on his face or feel bloody responsible. Not tonight.

Daniel cast about for salvation and found it seated across from him.

What did Thea like?

Byron, he recalled from dinner, with an automatic twist of his lips. Poetry. Something he'd learned early and well to detest. Especially from poets whose names began with "B".

Byron...*Blake*. For those, he held a particular abhorrence.

William Blake, the word-wielding rascal, had gifted Daniel's father with a rare volume of his works. A volume his sire revered but that he and his twin thought better suited to post chamber-pot wiping than recreational reading.

Sadly though, young boys had little say in their education especially when their elders held a particular engraver-turned-poet in high esteem. As a consequence, their childhood tutor forced him and David to study and recite the lines *ad nauseam*. To this day, Daniel regretted how he could not block them from his memory.

He was *not* a "Little Boy Lost", by damn! Neither was he a man who needed to moderate his bloody passions!

But damn his infernal curiosity, he did want to know more about his new mistress.

Did she have a bonnet collection numbering upwards of thirty-seven? Did she waste considerable time cataloging baubles enough to fill fourteen jewelry cases? (Nay, for she wore not a single one upon her plainly dressed person.) What of butterflies? Was she, perhaps, enamored of their wing colors?

Enamored to a sufficient degree to spike a pin through their hearts and tack them in a padded box? To retrieve and carry with her a broken, iridescent wing and tell the milliner *that*, precisely, was to be the exact shade of the ribbons on her next bonnet?

All atrocities his former, fancifully dressed fancy piece had indulged in.

Daniel couldn't see it, none of it. Not from Thea, the composed, if absurdly, *annoyingly* quiet woman across from him. But by God, he wanted to *hear* it from her lips.

So he pried his open. "Tell me of yourself."

She jumped as though a cannon blasted from his mouth.

"What would you know?" she said after recovering her composure. "You have but to ask and I am pleased to share, though I fear you will find me an uninspiring topic."

She was wrong, so very wrong.

Daniel thought a moment, determining the best way to inquire without revealing his weakness. No longer could he expect rescue from a top-jiggling trollop. "How long ago were you widowed?"

Now that was brilliant. First question he poses is about the other man most recently in her life? Hell, he might as well have asked her if her husband was a good lover.

He bit his tongue to still the plethora of other thoughts yearning to break free. *Had* her spouse been a good lover? Was there anything she particularly enjoyed in the bedchamber? Anything she wished to avoid? Would she, perchance, be amenable to amorous convincing, should the need arise? (His need had arisen, achingly so, now that she was close and they were alone.)

"Just over a year, my lord."

A year what? His mind blanked, too busy conjuring thoughts of her splayed across his big bed.

Daniel ground his teeth and cast about for another query, minus any troublesome letters.

"We were married nearly eight," she saved his tooth enamel by offering. "I knew Mr. Hurwell most of my life. He and my father were friends."

Which told him much. He and her *father* were friends.

Not her.

As though she'd shared more than she meant to, Thea's eyes sought the closed curtain. Her hands fidgeted—a flurry of movement that wound his gut tighter than the strings of her reticule.

Hurwell. Hurwell. *Mr. Hurwell.* Why did that name sound familiar? Why did his mouth burst out with, "So it-it wasn't a love match?"

She mashed those lovely lips together before freeing them to say, "Nay. 'Twas a match of convenience. *Their* convenience. My father and Mr. Hurwell's, that is. When Papa fell ill, he urged me to accept the proposal, which had been repeated more than once. I finally did so, to give him some reassurance at the end."

She was talking now, which was all very well and good but not at all what he wanted to hear.

The gulf between them threatened to widen, from a carriage to a chasm. "It won't do."

His deep, gravelly murmur surprised them both. She gasped at his intensity; he smiled because it came forth without hesitation.

"What won't, my lord?"

"This...ah..." Regardless of the convenience of making her his convenient (which made him no better than her deceased husband, he realized on a groan), he was curious about Thea, about her past, her dreams. About her missing coat. *About what lay beneath the drab olive gown.* It won't do. Nay, not at all! "This..." Divide? Distance? "*Space* between us. Won't...suffice."

The exposed skin of her neck beckoned once more. Would it be as cold as the air between them or, if Ellie's bewitching cream had truly blessed him, hot like passion?

The seats creaked as he rose and transferred to the one she occupied. Her startled glance flittered away. He wasted no time stripping off his gloves. With one hand, he covered the tangled fingers in her lap. With the other, he cupped her cheek and turned her to face him.

Warm. Even in the cold night air, her skin was heated, giving him his answer. *Passion.* No frigid miss could have skin this warm.

He bent his head to press his lips to hers and the fingers beneath his tightened further.

Giving in to his body's urging, he opened his mouth and slid his tongue over her lips.

She jerked back with a gasp, staring at him with overly bright eyes. A sharp trembling besieged her limbs.

His heart sank.

If she scared this easily at his touch, how was he

supposed to bed her?

He wasn't in the habit of supplying lodgings for just any female off the street. Neither could he imagine taking his pleasure with someone who shrank from his touch.

Sliding his hand from her face, the other from her lap, he leaned back against the seat and expelled a breath. Then another. He turned his head, eyes seeking hers, expecting condemnation. Instead, finding only her outline, the interior lantern having burnt down to fumes.

He unclenched his jaw to inquire, as silkily as he could manage—no need to scare her further—"Problem?"

She'd raised a hand to her mouth. He saw a hint of her fine, pale glove when she lowered it to her throat. "What-what do you mean?"

"Is there a...prob...blem?" He waited a moment. When she didn't respond, he clarified, "With my t-t—" *Deep breath, Daniel,* he remembered his grandfather saying, *the words will come when they're ready.* Well dammit, he needed them ready now. "You have issues with my...touch?"

"Nay!" she said emphatically, convincingly. "Not at all. I, um...ah..." The hand at her neck took to fanning her face, tiny, panicky puffs of air he felt a foot away. "I'm not used to kisses such as yours."

Gad. Even his kisses were wrong. Too passionate? he wondered and then discounted the insane notion. He'd barely touched her.

Despite his attraction, he was becoming

concerned. If she couldn't stomach his kisses, how would she tolerate his cock? "What t-t-type of kisses are you used to?"

"Are you laughing at me?" She sounded stiff, hurt by the thought.

"Laughing? At you? *Never.*" When she remained defensively quiet, he ordered, "Thea. Answer me."

How else would he know how to please her?

"None at all. I'm not used to any manner of kiss." The words were a shameful whisper, one that lashed at his conscience for demanding she admit it. But he couldn't regret the urge when she tore off one glove and gripped his hand, halting his retreat back across the squabs. "Pray, do not fault me for the lack," she implored into the shadows between them. "I've not had ample opportunity to receive nor bestow such affection."

Ample opportunity? "Oh?"

"*Your* kiss—'twas not unpleasant, only unexpected. I..."

When the lantern flame flickered and faltered, fizzled to nothing, she clutched him harder—the hand that hadn't suffered a mangling previously—and Daniel sensed she was winding up to confess all under the cover of darkness. "Earlier tonight, I watched Lord Big No—*ahem*, Lord Donaldson—lick...ah, *intimate* parts of his partner, but I failed to consider your tongue questing upon my mouth. Silly of me, I know." Her laugh was self-mocking. "It was my omission. I do apologize."

Her fingers pulled at his, but he was too startled

by the halting revelations to do more than enjoy the way she plucked at the naked skin of his palm while she haltingly said, "Please be assured, and I mean this most sincerely, Lord Tremayne, you may feel at liberty to place it there again."

It? His tongue? She invited him to place it upon her mouth?

Though beyond tempted, he had to clarify, "What 'intimate p-parts' exactly?"

"You knave!" A muffled giggle escaped as she tossed his hand from her. "Now I know I hear laughter in your voice."

She heard laughter when he felt lunacy? That would do. Would do famously. "Nay, 'tis curiosity."

"'Tis most ungentlemanly of you," she accused with breathless abandon, "to mock my ignorance thus."

'Twas most ungentlemanly of him to delight in her admitted ignorance but he did, oh how he did. So he told her. "You de-delight me."

"I delight your funny bone, you mean."

It was true.

He found, the more they bantered in the blackness, that he *was* suppressing laughter. What a freeing experience. "T-tell me"—he fisted the recently abandoned fingers to keep from groping her in the dark—"if not your m-m-mouth, where d-did you consider my...tongue upon your person?"

The perplexing widow (Was she one *in truth*—in the fleshly sense? Had her horse's arse of a husband truly *never* kissed her?) refused to answer what

Daniel most avidly wanted to hear. Although what she did next was infinitely better: she blindly raised her ungloved hand to his cheek, skimming it up his chest to map the way. He swallowed thickly when her fingers glided up his neck and again when they settled upon him.

She feathered her thumb across his lips and he felt the imprint of each individual finger cupping his jaw as she guided his head down while lifting hers.

Their lips touched a second later.

This time he kept his tongue to himself, wanting to see how *she* might kiss, given ample opportunity (which he had every intention of supplying her, every chance he could). In fact, he was more than willing to let her experiment on him, as much as she wanted, as long as he could entice her.

"Whoa. Whoa now!" Roskins brought the horses to a decisive stop. Their bodies lurched in tandem with the carriage. "We're here, milord."

Damn.

Did their mouths cling, reluctant to part, or was that mere folly on his part? A breath later, her lips were gone. The hand on his jaw flexed, then fled.

Thea edged away with a tiny whimper.

Of what? Frustration—that they weren't continuing? Fear—of him? Of what awaited her in the townhouse he'd procured?

What *did* she feel at the too-brief kiss? Irritation it hadn't deepened or relief at the interruption?

Daniel knew what he felt—twenty stone of pure lust. Another forty of regret—that he hadn't claimed her lips sooner, as in the second they'd entered the carriage.

When he moved to open the door, Thea stayed his arm. All humor had fled from her when she spoke. "Please. Do not hold my lack of experience in mistressing arts against me." *Mistressing arts?* "I remain very aware of the honor you do me, granting me the chance to please you. And once we arrive inside"—her voice cracked, giving lie to her words—"I'm ready for you to take me, my lord."

6

TAWDRY OR TITILLATING? 'TIS A MATTER OF OPINION...

UNCERTAIN AS TO the protocol for one in her position, Thea stood just inside the door of her new home. Upon first glimpse, she could tell it was grander than any place she'd lived.

Grander and golder and, well, *gaudier*. And she absolutely loved it.

The lower walls were painted a rich scarlet; above the wainscoting, they glimmered bronze in the flickering wall sconces. Flush against one wall and flanked by two ornate chairs, a rectangular table was draped with a red and bronze, fringe-trimmed brocade. Several ceramic figurines cavorted on one side of the table (carnally, if she wasn't mistaken) and a gleaming oval tray occupied the other, its polished surface conspicuously empty. Awaiting her correspondence?

How very indulgent!

The unexpected décor lent an opulent feel to the very air. Inhaling the lavish scents of decadence and relief—had she ever been privy to such a sumptuous, *safe* home?—Thea paused at the table to remove her remaining glove, placing the pair near the glittering tray.

Above the table, an arched mirror reflected her pale face and drab dress, along with two coordinating paintings on the opposite wall—her escort had stalled in front of one—each showing a voluptuous, artfully nude female in a very suggestive pose. Thea found it easier to focus on those wicked images rather than her own plain one.

The resplendent, if debauched, excess—from the obscene figures to the stark naked models adorning her new walls—were the exact opposite of the pallid squalor she'd been reduced to the last few months. Naughty or not, Thea knew a home this splendid surely boasted more than moldy potatoes in the larder.

And that made it very fine indeed.

After shedding his coat and slinging it over the arm of one chair, Lord Tremayne came up behind her and caught her gaze in the mirror. He placed his warm hand low across her back and cleared his throat. "Not what I—"

He choked off what sounded like a curse and his fingers flexed just above her hip. The added pressure incited a tremor that quaked through her legs and down to her toes. Thea's feet stretched in the cold slippers as heat blossomed.

"I like it," she said before he could deride her new abode, turning against his large form to look up and capture his gaze directly. "I like it exceedingly. It's more beautiful than I imagined." And to think—she'd only seen the entryway!

He grunted—and slid his hand a bit lower.

Her breath caught in her throat but then a strident bird cry arrested her attention and his hand fell away when he stepped back.

Cuckoo—cuckoo—cuckoo...

Through twelve interminable seconds, they both stood transfixed. Because instead of a sweet (or annoying) chirping bird extending out and bobbing sprightly, their eyes were greeted with two figures, one unmistakably male, the other female. Female *and* on her knees, mouth open and bobbing over his...er...um...

"Gracious me," Thea said when she could garner a breath. "That's...that's..."

"Filthy."

His ragged growl drew her gaze away from the clock. Was that embarrassment flushing the tips of his ears?

Thea's eyes darted over the portraits, the figurines, the cuckoo clock, and finally settled on the man in front of her.

"I was thinking funny," she said lightly. "Wretchedly funny."

The dark scowl faded to be replaced by a slow and knowing grin. "Funny? Aye, Thea, we'll...d-do—" He broke off on a slight cough, muffled quickly by his fist. "Shall we?"

Extending his arm, he indicated the prominent staircase that stood off to the right. If this townhouse was arranged as most, the split stairway led down to the kitchen and up to the bedchambers.

Thea nodded and he gestured for her to precede him, placing one hand on her waist as their feet followed the ascending path of the crimson runner. Though acutely aware of the gentle pressure of his fingers curved near her hip, Thea had to bite back a laugh.

If a scant hour in his company had taught her that mayhap she didn't hate *every* cuckoo clock, what other surprising revelations might her new association bring?

AT THE TOP LANDING, only one door stood ajar. Lord Tremayne steered her toward it.

"My, how lovely and-and—" She gasped, stumbling to a stop just over the threshold, barely muting her *monstrously huge*. Without doubt, this chamber alone had to be the size of the entire living quarters above the clock shop.

With none of the ostentation found below, the elegant cream-and-pink room possessed beautifully carved furniture. Painted roses trailing on vines decorated each piece of the matching set: armoire, a dresser along one wall, and a pair of chairs at a circular table occupying a corner.

There were few adornments beyond the furniture itself, simply the large bed, a vase of real roses atop the armoire—how extravagant—and lit candles sprinkled liberally throughout—how doubly extravagant.

As he hovered closer, Lord Tremayne's heat scorched along her back. Under his direction, Thea stepped farther into her new room.

"May I have a moment of privacy?" she asked, surreptitiously looking for the chamber pot.

He indicated a shadowed door across the expanse. "I…believe what you seek is through there."

"I'll hurry," she promised, edging toward what she realized was an adjacent dressing room. "Just please, ah…give me a moment—"

"Thea." He held up one hand and gestured between them and then to the bed, his gaze never leaving hers. "This is…not a race."

"Then I won't hurry," she assured him. At his raised eyebrow, she blurted, "But neither will I dally."

Her cheeks heated at the amused look he gave her and Thea rushed to the promised respite, swiftly shutting the door behind her.

Only to find the windowless room completely dark.

Completely, as in pitch-black.

She blinked and waited—to no avail. She wouldn't have known if a herd of mice were juggling grapes at her feet.

Thea eased the door open. Lord Tremayne

hadn't moved. "A candle—" She pointed as she sped toward the closest one. "I'm afraid I need it."

"B-by all means." The wretch was laughing at her again, but she couldn't seem to mind, not when his eyes twinkled too. He clasped his hands behind his back, and when she raced past him again, candle in hand, he winked.

Face flaming, body thrumming, Thea escaped to the sanctuary of the dressing room where she found not only the chamber pot but also a basin of water and more personal necessities than she knew what to do with. And, unmistakably, what she was expected to don for the night—a long, ivory gown hanging next to the washstand.

Knowing she mustn't tarry, she quickly disrobed and took care of her ablutions. Rather than linger over the task, one made especially pleasant by the warmed water and soft towel, Thea made do with as expeditious a cleaning as she could muster, ever aware of the strapping six foot plus of utter masculinity waiting only a few paces away.

Once her skin fairly sizzled from the brisk scrubbing, she reached for the voluminous night rail. "Heavens, there's enough fabric here to sail the Royal Navy."

Shouldn't official Mistress Apparel be more...scant?

Thea laughed at herself. What had she expected? To be attired as the buxom beauties in the paintings downstairs—in absolutely nothing at all?

"You noddy! Be grateful for the long sleeves that'll hide the bruises!"

That fortified her and she pulled the gown over her head, inhaling in surprise when the filmy fabric caressed her bare skin. Practically choking when she realized the wealth of froth was in direct opposition to what it concealed—or didn't conceal.

Every shadow and cleft of her body was more than apparent. But before she had time to wither in mortification, Thea saw how the waves of diaphanous fabric hinted at curves and a womanly softness she knew had long deserted her limbs thanks to the meager rations she'd come to subsist on.

The capacious gown had obviously been sewn for a woman much taller than she. The neckline rode low on her shoulders, the sleeves hung inches past her fingertips, the hem pooled on the floor, but the nearly transparent mistresswear only enticed Thea to stand tall. (It was either that or bemoan her lack of needle and thread, and she'd never been one for moaning over what couldn't be changed.)

It was past time to begin "earning" the right to her new accommodations and the lovely night-clothes. If she spent any more time *thinking* about what she'd be doing in the next few minutes—with a man she'd only just met—she'd likely barricade the door and that wouldn't do, not at all.

Done with dithering, she leaned over to blow out the candle. As the smoke wafted by her in the dark,

Thea decided she must learn to conduct herself as someone used to such lavish surroundings.

That thought fortifying her courage, Thea bunched the lacy cuffs in her fists, held the overlong gown off the floor so she wouldn't trip, took a deep breath for courage and barreled through the door. "I'm ready, my lord."

THANK GOD. The avocado abomination she called a dress had been abandoned in favor of an alluring night rail.

She'd left her hair pinned in place, but the provocative confection she emerged in more than made up for it, a confection he'd happily appreciate —off her—at a later date.

At the moment, damn his infernal luck, he had a bravely trembling mistress-to-be to soothe.

For despite what she claimed, he knew better. She wasn't ready. Nowhere close.

She might not be a stranger to sex, but she was definitely a stranger to kissing. And to sex *with him*, and he'd be damned if he'd "rush his fences" and ruin a potentially grand thing.

Striving for control he was far from feeling, Daniel allowed his attention to drift over her shoulder to the door she'd burst from. He'd hoped the time alone might work a miracle, that her inhibitions, along with her ratty dress, might be cast onto the coals upon her return. But judging by the quickness of her breaths, the shaking of her person, that was too much to wish for, at least for tonight.

While she'd been gone, he'd taken a moment to appreciate the scrupulously clean environment. The furnishings below stairs—and in the master chamber down the hall, he'd noted when he'd escaped to find his own chamber pot—were tawdry beyond belief.

But the couple his man of affairs had hired to staff the place promised to make up for the prior occupant's lack of taste. They knew their duties: the chamber was cozy from the banked fire, the bed was turned down (in here, not the master's rooms he noticed; seemed he wasn't the only one who found the garish vulgarity off-putting, given how *this* was the room they'd readied). The perfect number of candles were lit—enough to see by but not so many the intimacy was shattered.

Add to that, they knew how to disappear—he knew they resided in the servants' quarters on the lowest floor, but he hadn't heard a peep.

Thea's "I'm ready," shook him from his stupor.

What was he to do with her? Or with the need filling his loins?

THEA SKIDDED to a halt at the sight of Lord Tremayne standing patiently near the bed.

He was fully clothed save for his tailcoat, which he'd draped over the dainty bench at the foot of the massive bed.

At her appearance, pleasure flared in his eyes but the look was squelched so quickly she wondered if she mistook his approval.

Would he stay the night? Sleep here after her mistress duties were done? She'd lain in the same bed nightly with Mr. Hurwell and it had been a singularly...uneventful experience. Unless actually copulating, her late husband had taken pains to remain on his side—and instructed her to do the same (the one time she'd drifted near, Mr. Hurwell had taken exception to her "cold extremities" upon his person).

Lord Tremayne didn't seem a man to be put off by frigid feet. Though, Thea reflected, curling her toes into the thick rug, they didn't feel the least bit cold now.

What to do? What to do?

Her fingers clenched the delicate fabric and she made a conscious effort to relax. Tossing her head as though she did this sort of thing every night, she repeated, "I am ready, my lord."

Ready for what, she wasn't quite sure.

Him to kiss her again, certainly.

"On the...bed." Lord Tremayne spoke the command quietly.

Having him tell her what to do was a relief. Thinking mayhap he'd kiss her there, she crossed the room under his watchful gaze.

The bed itself was fit for royalty, standing far above the floral rug and supporting a sumptuous mattress. Thea marveled at her new circumstance as she perched warily upon the edge and ran her fingertips over the crisp sheets. Amazing, from sleeping on rags piled on the floor to this? Pristine and unwrinkled, the linens bespoke of purity. A whimsical notion, yet not sufficient to detour her thoughts from the direction they'd gone all evening...

What kind of lover would Lord Tremayne be? Slow and tender as she'd dreamed of as a girl, spinning fantasies about her future husband? Or abruptly efficient as Mr. Hurwell had been? Or possibly masterful and commanding as she longed for several years into her lackluster marriage?

Anything other than the tepid, perfunctory matings she'd known would suffice. It seemed Mr. Hurwell had thought it his duty to have congress with her monthly, whether he wished it or not. More than once, he'd even fallen asleep in the middle of the act—was it any wonder she'd questioned her ability to seduce and satisfy?

Thea sensed Lord Tremayne evaluating her and left off admiring the sheets to gaze up at the man she was here to please. Was he? Pleased at the sight of her? At the notion of bedding her?

Brooding silence aside, she hadn't a clue.

He stood near the foot of the bed, his formidable shoulders slightly hunched, fists clenched, staring at her and not looking very much like a man pleased.

But also definitely *not* on the verge of sleep. Quite the opposite, in fact. He studied her with an intensity she might find alarming from anyone else.

But there was no mistaking how her body responded to him, growing restless in the strangest places... "Lord Tremayne? My wish..."

She couldn't hold his gaze a moment more, so she looked down and was reminded how prominently the sheer gown displayed the summits of her breasts, the shadowed triangle between her thighs.

Shocking—how this much loose fabric managed to reveal. Shocking, that the sight of her nearly nude body didn't send her scurrying for cover but instead gave her a measure of confidence she'd lacked moments before.

She risked another glance at him. Surely, even in the dim candlelight, he could see her beaded nipples through the thin fabric. See how she didn't shrink from him. See how she was agreeable to pressing forward. Then why did he not move toward her? Take what he'd bought, what she freely offered?

Was he waiting for her to lie back amid the fluffy bedcovers? Waiting for her to crawl beneath them? Or, mayhap, the opposite?

Think like a mistress. "I wish to please you. Shall I"—*gulp*—"remove my gown?"

"NAY. LEAVE IT."

For if she didn't, Daniel feared he'd pounce on her and banish to the rubbish bin his good and wholesome intentions of giving her time. In truth, he was of two minds—take her anyway, despite Sarah's counsel, or depart Temptation's presence.

Return home and palm his staff as he'd been doing nightly, only this time, to the vision of Thea.

What circumstances brought her to this place? Because it assuredly wasn't an honest desire to barter her body, not the way she trembled more than a leaf in a storm.

He half-wished he hadn't snapped when Penry dangled the bait. Thea was a young, fresh-faced guppy swimming in shark-infested waters, not at all the experienced, older widow he'd been led to believe.

He ought to cut his line and throw her back.

Daniel's tongue pressed against the roof of his mouth as their too-brief kiss flashed through his mind. He wanted to taste her again—everywhere. *Everywhere.*

If he tossed her overboard, someone else would catch her up.

The thought of anyone else swimming in her waters— "God-d-d-*dammit!*"

Thea jumped a foot and Daniel realized he'd cursed out loud. His infernal mouth!

"My lord?" Her face was flushed and her body quaked as though the bed balanced on a high wire. But her eyes, those soft, mossy eyes met his valiantly, as if she didn't abhor the thought of him taking her. As if she was amenable to it, mayhap even anticipated it with something other than dread, but she wasn't *comfortable* with the idea.

Not with him. Not yet.

And when she gave a solemn blink and a hint of

hurt entered those pretty eyes, as though she sensed his hesitation and had concluded he found her lacking (patently preposterous!), it all caught up with him: the whole entire aggravating day...

Wylde's asinine request, Ellie's tears, the damn orrery he couldn't get working. Add in the weeks of sexual frustration, his own agonizing over Sarah's "party" and meeting a potential mistress...

Tom Everson.

And there it was. The one thing troubling him more than anything else—save for Thea's trembling—how effectively he'd crushed the young man's spirit.

Bloody hell.

Bloody, bloody hell! Where was the ease a man's mistress promised? The refuge from life's travails? The night of *sleep*?

By God, he'd paid for the right to use her body and use it he would!

And it had nothing to do with that wounded look in her eyes. *Nothing.*

"T-turn over." Even a paltry two-word request was beyond him? Double dammit!

"Pardon?" He could tell he'd startled her.

Too damn bad. "Over," he ordered harshly, gesturing with his arm, sick of dithering. "On your stomach."

Confusion wrinkling her brow, she complied, bringing her legs to the mattress and then rolling to face the bed. He took advantage of the moment to prowl the edges of the room and extinguish every candle save the one burning closest to her bed.

Mayhap the shadows would help alleviate her nerves.

They sure as hell didn't mitigate his desire, not when he returned to her side and found her resting on bent elbows, upper body propped over a pillow.

She didn't look at him, didn't ask what he had planned, just resolutely waited.

Waited for him to join her, to take her.

Well, take her he would—*his* way. The lewd way he'd begun envisaging after his former mistress dragged him to one of those wretched shadow plays which illustrated the arousing act in all its unnatural glory. The bawdy way the same former mistress had permitted a time or two—just enough to whet Daniel's appetite for more.

Thump. His left boot hit the floor.

Snarl and *thump*, he wrenched the right one off as well. Then he tore through the buttons on his trousers and pushed them and his drawers down, kicked them off.

He was stiff as a pike, his poker ready to *poke* but damn him if he'd settle for *resolute*. No, by God, when he finally took his *new* mistress, really took her as a man did a woman, it'd be because Thea *wanted* him to. Needed him to release the torrent of desire he'd build into a writhing ache...

But not tonight. Tonight was for him. To ease *his* relentless desire

The mattress dipped when he placed one knee

near her hip. And because he couldn't wait any longer, Daniel smoothed the night rail over the small of her back and the flare of her hip. Savoring how the material felt sliding over her warm skin, he lowered his open palm to the swell of her backside, settling it firmly atop the cheek closest to him. She made a faint sound in her throat, not a whimper, not a protest (he didn't think), perhaps something between the two.

He wanted to ask her. Wanted to haul her upright, take her hand in his and *talk*. Ask her if she feared him (and assure her she needn't), ask why Sarah had issued that blasted caution, why circumstances had dictated a change in her fortune (because that...that...that maggoty dress had no business covering the form of such a well-mannered young woman).

He wanted to ask her whether he could stay the night—and where the blazes was her cloak.

But Daniel knew better than he did his own name if he opened his mouth and started the imbecilic spewing before he ever had a chance to give her a different impression first, all would be lost.

Just as he was lost—lost to reason and any finer sense when he watched his fingers travel downward over her legs until they gripped the hem of the frothy night rail and, by a will stronger than his own, whipped it up her body until the fabric ballooned at her waist. So his eyes could drink her in.

The gentle flare of womanly thighs, the anxiously flexing toes and muscles of her calves, the sweetest little *derrière*—clenched so tight he couldn't mistake how appalled she must be, knowing he looked his fill.

Relax, he murmured in his mind, shifting the rest of his weight onto the bed and straddling her thighs as both his hands stroked the halves of her arse.

His heart gave an unfamiliar lurch when she let him, her ragged breaths the only sign of her distress. That dark seam between his fingers beckoned, especially now that she'd unclenched, and Daniel edged his thumbs inward, beyond pleased when her hips tilted as though inviting him to explore further...to delve into deeper, damper territory.

But his own territory had grown damp—the small circular spot darkening the tail of his shirt where it drifted past the tip of his rod glaring the evidence. His cock was past ready to spend.

Without giving himself time to debate further, Daniel firmed his grip on her cheeks and slid the opposing sides of her bum apart, groaning at the musky, dark pink flesh the action exposed.

WHAT WAS he *doing* back there?

"Ah..." Thea gulped down the apprehension threatening to close off her air. She was a grown woman. She'd had amorous congress before, she consoled her growing nerves.

But not like this!

Never like this!

She trusted him, Thea reminded herself. Trusted

the understanding man in the carriage who had kissed her so tenderly.

But still! "Lord Tremayne?"

With his broad hands holding her posterior in a most objectionable way, his heavy and hot lower half hovering over hers, Thea's insides were a pure muddle.

Outrage, uncertainty, perhaps a bit of passion in the mix, it all boiled together, churning her stomach in a most disturbing manner. She strove to look over her shoulder. "What, ah, are you—"

"Hush," he growled, lowering himself on top of her. At the first feel of his erect male length against the sensitive cheeks of her bottom (*between* them actually!), Thea felt her hips flinch away, then press up to meet him. Her mind might be screaming protests, but it seemed her traitorous low country had other thoughts.

Without further ado, his long legs blanketed hers and his upper body settled over her back. He arranged his arms around hers, bracing the bulk of his weight on his elbows, and cradled her fisted hands within his large palms. Large, strong hands she couldn't help but stare at, their heat seeping through her skin and igniting an unfamiliar sizzle in her belly.

Hands, thank heavens, that were no longer groping her posterior.

Though why that reality gave her a pang of disappointment instead of relief, Thea couldn't have said, not now, not when so many new sensations were bombarding her nerve endings.

Her breath—what she could catch of it—came in tiny pants.

When he nuzzled his cheek next to hers, she caught the subtle aroma of the wine he'd consumed with dinner. That and, now that he surrounded her, the elusive, sweetly spicy scent, the one so uniquely his. And an understated reminder of the outdoors, pine or juniper perhaps. Again she thought of the aborted kisses they'd exchanged in the carriage.

Kiss me again.

But she couldn't ask, not when he'd just told her to hush.

As though he couldn't be bothered to remove it, he still wore his shirt. Her eyes fixed on the cream-colored linen blending with the gossamer sleeves of her gown as he relaxed his weight against her and started to move, that part of him rubbing so insidiously, so illicitly between the crease made by the lobes of her bottom.

The deliberate motions of him burrowing along the crevice pressed her deeper into the bed. Rather than give in to maidenly hysteria (her first inclination, which was definitely not appropriate Mistress Behavior), Thea concentrated on the masculine hands bracketing hers, the knuckles raised and rough-looking, and tried not to think about how gently those hands had just caressed her in such a personal place. Tried not to think about the foreign texture of his groin snugged flush against her posterior.

Devil take her to Devonshire, it proved impossible.

How could one *not* think about something so intolerably titillating, so very wickedly stimulating? Especially when a curious tingling began in her abdomen, one she'd felt a time or two but never quite this strongly.

She wanted to roll over, to curve her legs around his and hug him to her. To experience his bare chest pressed against hers, to feel the full weight of him as she looked into his stormy, amber eyes. Despite her misgivings, Thea positively had to express that desire. "Lord Tremayne, I—"

"Shhhht!" It was a grunt this time but he softened it by kissing behind her ear. A lingering kiss that moved leisurely down her neck and stopped when confronted by the lacy edge of the night rail.

He reached between them to pull the neckline lower. The delicate lace resisted and several threads snapped.

"D-damn me," he muttered between kisses. "Buy you another." And then his lips plastered themselves to the groove between her neck and shoulder and he kissed her with more feeling. Her head dropped to rest on his bent arm as she surrendered her inhibitions to the divine assault of his mouth.

His legs slid between hers, forcing them to part. The action widened her thighs and slanted her intimately into the mattress. His thrusting motions continued, prompting Thea to squeeze the halves of her bottom together. For if she didn't, he might slip and accidentally enter her—*there*.

The fast motion of his pelvis rocking into her became hard to follow. Confused beyond reckoning, Thea simply held on, enduring the irregular position, enjoying his kisses, wondering...

Didn't he want to be *inside* her? To put his long stalk in her delicate flower? Mr. Hurwell had used those words once, early in their marriage. She'd not paid them much mind then.

But now, she sensed her flower pearling with dew, preparing to bloom. If only Lord Tremayne would—

He gripped her hands tighter as his breathing became erratic. His weight bore down and her hips began to rotate on their own, to move against the mattress, angling so that the bed provided friction to her center, even as her traitorous backside pressed up into Lord Tremayne's groin. Giving herself up to the moment, Thea rode the waves of his undulating body, consciously relaxing in order to move in tandem with him.

"Thea." Another grunt, the whisper of her name, but one that touched her. She might be perplexed by his unexpected actions, but she felt unaccountably cherished by the way he said it.

He stopped kissing her shoulder and exhaled harshly near her ear. A drop of sweat rolled off his face and landed on the bed sheet. Again he rasped, "Thea."

His side whiskers rubbed against her temple, abrading her skin, when he said it.

The force of his movements increased. His hips jerked hard into her several times before stilling. And Thea knew the warmth of his seed upon her back.

Other than a slight twitch of his spent erection, all was frozen: time, her pounding heart, even the restless yearning centered in her woman's flesh.

He shifted against her and his long exhalation stirred the loosened hair near her ear.

Would he tell her to face him? To roll beneath him? Would he now thrust into her rose? End the persisting ache in her abdomen?

Anticipation wound through her.

Abruptly, he released her fingers, pushing up on his arms and away from her. He eased off her bottom. The air hit her newly exposed skin and caused chills to erupt along her spine. The sticky wetness remained on her back.

"Lie still," he commanded, climbing from the bed.

Thea had to stifle a giggle. What did he think she might do? Offer to rush downstairs and bring him a brandy? Jump up and dance a quadrille?

As soon as it formed, she longed to share the jest with him. But the wall of silence he'd erected stayed her tongue. Wondering what would come next, she held her breath as he stepped into the dressing room.

While she awaited his return, she repeatedly

smoothed the sheet beneath her fingers, searching out the spot where his drop of perspiration had landed. The simple motion calmed her, though the wetness remained elusive.

Seconds later, Lord Tremayne approached the side of the bed. He ran a cloth over her lower back and bum, even swiping once between her cheeks!

Now would he come back and join her? Finish the act?

Aye, for she heard him removing his shirt. A sigh of relief, of nervous excitement escaped as Thea languidly rolled to her side—only to find him pulling his shirt not *off* but his trousers *on*.

"Lord Tremayne?" Thea hurriedly lowered the night rail and spun to her back. She hugged a pillow to her torso, vexed to see his attention focused on his garments—and not his mistress. Why, now that he'd finished their erotic exchange, he wouldn't even look at her! Was too enamored with wrestling his tailcoat after snatching it from the bench.

"My lord? You're leav*ing*?" Her voice squeaked at the last, making her sound needy indeed.

Definitely not the impression she intended to give her new benefactor. "Of course, you must leave." She attempted a credible, casual laugh (and feared she failed miserably). "You have a home to return to, after all."

A home he likely shared with a *wife*.

Thea nearly choked on that unpalatable thought. Why had she not thought to ask Sarah?

After all, Lord Penry was married. Chances were Lord Tremayne was too.

Emotions too plentiful to name, too punishing to endure threatened her outward calm but Thea resolutely shrugged them off. *Dwell on him, you ninny, and your new* safe *existence.* "Thank you again for providing me such beautiful accommodations and —and—"

Why did her throat thicken and the words come swiftly, as though trying to outrun tears? Why were the carnal urges storming her insides stronger than ever before? She barely knew the man, knew even less *about* him. She only knew that she wanted to again feel his body upon hers, this time without the barrier of their clothing. To explore his broad chest, feel his skin, slick with sweat, against—

Thea sat up and clutched the pillow tighter. She'd put on a confident air or her name wasn't Dorothea Jane Hurwell, the dashed Best Mistress of 1815!

DANIEL KNEW HIS DUTY.

Send the woman a bauble first thing tomorrow. A sparkly trinket delivered straight from the jeweler's with his name attached to the box.

That's what men did for their mistresses—the requisite token of appreciation; something tangible, something expensive that paved the way for the next encounter.

Next encounter? Hell, he wasn't satisfied from *this* encounter. Not even close.

He might have melted across her back, gained some measure of release, but it wasn't the one he wanted—to mount her Venus mound and ride them both to heaven—nor the one he promised himself he'd take—

Damn his cowardly hide! He hadn't been able to do it—breach that virgin territory of hers. Not and maintain his honor. *Coitus per anum* might be well and good for a man's raunchy mistress, but Thea didn't act like one and he'd be damned if her first introduction to sex with him was an act of sodomy guaranteed to drown any tender feelings she might ever harbor for him before they had a chance to float to the surface.

Though he wanted to doff his vestments rather than don them and hunker down in that pretty, feminine bed, he didn't trust himself to exercise restraint if he stayed the night through.

Ignoring the inner promptings to linger, Daniel snagged his tailcoat from the bench and shoved his arm into it just like he shoved away his yearning —ruthlessly.

He might know his duty but the vague notions that brimmed in him now confused the hell out of him. Duty mixed with not-quite-filled desires and an odd eagerness to please. To convince Thea she'd made the right choice, choosing him as her protector.

Mayhap he'd compose a note, a sincere and personal "thank you" to accompany the trinket.

Pen her a missive? The asinine thought had his arm missing the second sleeve twice.

What was he thinking? He was a grown man with physical urges, not a damn suitor for her hand!

Never before had he thought to send a gift because he *wanted* to. He hadn't even left her bedchamber—and yet he was already acting like a lovesick swain, anticipating his return...

Pining for more time with her. A time when he might tup her properly.

A time when he might hold her, sleep with her in his arms... A time when he might stay the night.

He thought to kiss her, to stroke the fallen hair from her flushed face and tell her with the touch of his lips how much he *wanted* to stay. But he knew his own limits as well as his duty.

So, without sparing her another glance, he picked up his boots and crossed to the door. Hand on the knob, he stared at the dark wood in front of him. "Thea." Just the act of saying her name soothed the rasp plaguing his neck. "May I visit you again?"

"Certainly, my lord. You are welcome here anytime."

She answered too swiftly for him to mistake her reply. *Of course* she could do naught but agree. After all, it was his money buying the house. Buying *her*.

The tenor of their association gave her no other choice. His fingers tightened on the brass knob.

This wasn't how he wanted it! Not between them.

Risking a glance, he angled to catch her gaze. She looked so damn inviting, hair mussed, plump lips curved in a tremulous smile—one that didn't quite make it to her eyes and therefore kept his hand in place, strangling the knob, so he wouldn't lunge for her. That and the reddened patch the torn neckline revealed—where his damn whiskers had abraded her soft, soft skin. "Thea."

It was a sigh. An apology, a question. All he couldn't say.

One she answered simply with, "I will never turn away your company."

But would she welcome it?

When she offered, "In truth, I will eagerly await your next visit," words she needn't have uttered, his pride was soothed and he decided she just might.

Mayhap his earlier actions hadn't botched things beyond repair. "Very well."

He wanted to tell her how much she pleased him. How he'd enjoyed laughing with her in the carriage, holding her within the cage of his arms so very briefly. How he looked forward to more time with her alluring backside, more time with *her*.

But of course he could attempt none of those things, not with *his* damn mouth.

After a final, abrupt nod, he wrenched the door open and escaped.

NOW THAT SHE WAS ALONE, the finality of the latch clicking into place sounded disproportionately loud.

Thea was positive he'd wanted to say more before he plowed through the doorway. Twice, he'd opened his mouth but both times slammed it shut.

Had she displeased him? Nay, because he'd expressed his desire to return.

Releasing her worries on a sigh as she sank deep into the sumptuous mattress, Thea heard him pause outside the bedchamber to pull on his boots. A moment later, he pounded down the stairs.

So this was it? Her first night as a fallen woman. Curious how she felt so very *elevated*, then. So very—

He raised his voice, calling out. Thea cocked her head and heard the low rumble of conversation before Lord Tremayne exited the townhouse.

Afterward, someone shut the door and locked it —from inside.

Which could only mean that, in addition to securing the house, he'd also procured a servant? *For her?* Though in her youth she'd experienced such, since her marriage, Thea had learned to depend solely on herself, money for servants something Mr. Hurwell decried as an unnecessary luxury.

But now it seemed she had someone else to depend on. Goodness, that would take some getting used to. Time enough to greet them when she wasn't so befuzzled.

Perplexity over Lord Tremayne's disquieting behavior and excitement over her new lodgings battled in her breast.

Breasts that felt heavy and acutely sensitive.

She slid her fingers over their tips, still tight and

hard. Though she'd never touched herself outside of bathing before, Thea couldn't stop her growing curiosity. Given the added knowledge she had thanks to Sarah, the added awareness thanks to Lord—

What *was* his given name? "Lord Tremayne" seemed so inappropriately formal now.

Now that he'd awakened new urges.

Thea allowed one hand to wind down her stomach. When it reached the juncture of her legs, she pressed inward. Even through the gown, undeniable moisture greeted her fingertips. That and the insistent longing gripping her loins told her she'd *wanted* the sex act tonight.

It was more than she could have hoped for.

Tomorrow. How she hoped Lord Tremayne visited her tomorrow, for she ached to be with him again. To laugh with him again. To have him, not just on top of her, but *inside* her.

Of their own accord, her fingers delved farther into her cleft. Never before had she felt so saturated. Thea scrambled to raise the gown out of the way. When she did, the warm slickness covered her fingers as her inner muscles pulled them deep. With the palm of her hand, she rubbed against her core, flinching from the pressure.

Determined not to recoil, to brave the new sensations as she knew a Proper Mistress (what a combination!) ought, she moved her hand, pushing her fingers higher, and rocked her pelvis against her palm. Instead of bringing relief, the motions only heightened the ache.

Uncertain what to do next, feeling so tightly wound she wanted to burst, Thea eventually slowed the motions, then pulled her fingers free. She wiped them clean with the washcloth he'd left by the bed. Considerate man. She wished the bounder hadn't left.

At some point, she slept.

But only after counting the two hundred and forty-seven rose petals painted on the armoire (the remaining candle burned out before she could finish). And only after reaching the surprising realization that in addition to her body craving Lord Tremayne's return, her mind craved his company as well.

Though she was his, technically bought and paid for, when he looked at her, he didn't make her feel cheap or tawdry. Unlike the insulting glare of her former landlord, her new protector's gaze didn't brand her as his possession. Instead, being with him made her feel like a person. And a desirable one at that.

Gracious. She'd only just met the man and already felt indebted to him, thankful he'd given her something she hadn't even realized was missing these last difficult months—her dignity.

Thanks for reading *Mistress in the Making, Part 1 - SEDUCTIVE SILENCE*. If you have a chance to write a review, it's always appreciated. Reviews and word-of-mouth are two of the best things you can do for authors you enjoy.

Thea and Daniel are two of my all-time favorite characters. Their story is just getting started; turn the page for a look at ***Lusty Letters*** where they begin flirting and getting to know each other in a way I never expected when I handwrote Daniel's first missive to his new mistress. :)

For yourself, savor the silence when you can and speak up when you need to.

And keep an eye out for my *Roaring Rogues Regency Shapeshifters*, coming summer 2021!

LUSTY LETTERS EXCERPT

Chapter 1
Whereupon Things Progress Nicely…and Naughtily

Get posts and letters, and make friends with speed.

William Shakespeare, *King Henry IV*

The first attempt (the strip of paper it was on cut away, now balled up and swept to the floor):

Mrs. Hurwell–

What a horrid beginning. Did he *want* to instill more distance between them?

Second attempt:

Thea,
Please accept my most humble thanks—

"Humble thanks?" *What am I? Her deuced hat maker?*

Fourth attempt (currently being batted about by Cyclops, along with the other three):

Thea,
I count the hours until next we meet—

"Ballocks!" He wasn't ready to pen poetical-sounding odes to her either.

"Woof!" Cyclops agreed as yet another piece of crumpled paper was relegated to the empty grate.

Seventh (and final) attempt:

Thea,

Thank you for an enjoyable evening. I recalled someone mentioning you have a particular fondness for Byron. In all honesty, I cannot tolerate poetry (his or any others') so please accept this volume with my sincere wish that it brings you pleasure.

Until tonight.

Tremayne

Thea lifted her gaze from the missive to the servant who'd delivered it. Along with the note and a book of poems, he'd also handed her a bow-adorned box.

The spry young man had introduced himself as, "Buttons, miss, since I was caught eatin' one, with loads of others found missing. My papa told me once that our ma despaired but I don't remember, on account of being jus' months old at the time."

"What is etiquette in this regard?" she asked, smiling at the informative Buttons and gesturing toward the gifts and letter she now held. Thea hoped he knew—for she surely didn't. "Is Lord Tremayne expecting a reply?"

Not quite twenty, the youth was broad as a barn and twice as sturdy. His blunt-featured face was turned charming by the decisive cowlick that flipped up a good portion of his sandy-brown hair on the left side of his forehead. He'd told her, when he swiped the offending cowlick for the third time, that he had a twin, one whose hair misbehaved on the opposite side. "Expectin'? A reply?" He pondered a moment. "That I cannot say certain-like, but I do be thinkin' he might be hopin' fer one."

"Oh?"

"Aye." The young man dressed in formal livery stepped forward from his perch on the small landing just outside her townhouse. He tilted his head toward her ear, as though about to impart a confidence he didn't want her hovering new butler to overhear. "I was told to take my time in returnin'."

Assuming the ornate desk in the sumptuous drawing room was as well supplied as the rest of the residence, Thea was confident her eager fingers would have no trouble locating paper and ink. "Would you mind waiting in the kitchen while I compose one?"

She'd met the married couple hired to serve as caretakers and knew Mrs. Samuels was downstairs baking this very moment.

With a glance at Mr. Samuels, who had summoned Thea to the door once informed Lord Tremayne had requested his servant place the missive directly into her keeping, the spiffy footman stepped back a pace and diffidently crossed his arms behind his back, giving her a casual shake of his head. "I'll jus' wait here, ma'am. Take what time you need."

"Outside?" When intermittent rains thundered down for the second day in a row, making the uncovered porch damp and dreary? "Poppycock!"

A quick look at Mr. Samuels—and the nod he gave her—confirmed Thea's intuition, and she tugged the visiting servant over the threshold by one sleeve and pointed. "The kitchen is tucked at the back of that hallway, down the single flight of stairs. Mind you ask Mrs. Samuels to let you sample her lemon tarts."

When the young man smiled wider than the Thames, Thea suspected he had a fondness for baked goods. Either that or he'd caught sight of the painted nudes.

His next words illustrated how very wrong she was. "I'm right glad he found you, miss."

He being Lord Tremayne?

Well, of course. Who else could the footman mean? But to be told so directly—that a servant was glad his master had "found" *her*?

It was...unexpected, unusual.

It was flattering to the point that flutters abounded in her belly as Thea situated herself at the angled writing desk. She used the familiar task of readying the quill as she contemplated just what to say.

How did one answer the first note from their new protector? (Dare she hope it was the first of several?)

More importantly, how did she respond to the man who'd spent his seed on her back in the most intimate of acts but who hadn't spoken more than a paragraph to her all evening? And a paltry paragraph at that.

"Just reply to him as he addresses you," the words were out before she'd thought them through, echoing a semblance of Sarah's previous advice. "Same tone, same length."

Aye, that should suffice.

Thirty minutes later, a significant portion of which she'd wasted staring at the blank sheet, Thea had finally managed to fill it in, not quite to capacity but close. She wafted the page through the air, encouraging the ink to dry.

Lord Tremayne,

I delight in finding common ground, for despite public opinion to the contrary, I do not find much to appreciate in Byron. Based on the works I've read, he's overly dramatic for my tastes. Robert Burns, now, I adore and admit to a frisson (a small one, I assure you) of dismay at learning you hold no particular fondness for poetry. None at all? Are you quite certain? (I must clarify, you see, as it is something I find nearly incomprehensible.)

As to the volume you sent, I will treasure it always (are not gifts meant to be treasured?) though I will admit I am already in possession of this particular volume—and through no purchase of my own. I come to think mayhap Hatchards put it on sale?

Please, I beseech you, read the next few lines with your mind unfettered by past opinions:

Wee, sleekit, cow'rin, tim'rous beastie,
O, what a panic's in thy breastie!
Thou need na start awa sae hasty,
Wi' bickering brattle!

I wad be laith to rin an' chase thee,
Wi' murd'ring pattle!

Do these lines not speak to you? Are you not curious to know more? To learn the fate of this dear, wee beastie?

What of the incomparable Mr. William Shakespeare? Do you find anything in his work recommends itself to you? Oh, dear. I believe this must be a magical quill I employ for it has quite run away with my tongue. Do forgive me. (But here, I must interject: this new home I find myself situated in feels magical indeed. It is lovely. More serene than anywhere I've lived before. I do thank you, most sincerely. And will endeavor to please you in exchange.)

I anticipate tonight with a smile.

~~Dor~~ Thea

"Same tone, same *length*?" Bah. Brevity had never been one of her particular talents.

Frowning at herself, Thea folded the paper and sealed it with wax and the generic stamp she'd found in the desk. "You'd better hope that during the reading of it he doesn't nod off."

Daniel laughed and laughed again.

The demure little chit had taken him to task! That would teach him to deride all poetry in one unwarranted swoop.

And serene? She found that garish abode *serene*?

Another chuckle escaped.

He checked his pocket watch. It was scarce after 2:00 p.m. Hours yet until dark. Hours yet until he could feast his starved eyes on her again and see whether she was truly as lovely as he recalled.

"Rum fogged, I am," he muttered, reaching for another sheet.

Lusty Letters—Mistress in the Making, Part Two

Lusty Letters. For a man who hesitates over words isn't about to stumble over sentences, not when he has seduction on his mind.

Hampered by a pesky, persistent stammer, Lord Tremayne takes to writing letters when he decides to woo his new mistress, little realizing how their fun, flirty exchanges will quickly become the light of his day. Or how wretched he'll feel when the charming

Thea suggests they banter *in person*, possibly pen poetry—together. Blazing ballocks! Is she insane?

Her fascinating new protector has secrets—several. And though Thea fears losing her common sense—but never her heart—to the powerfully built Marquis, she stifles her longing to know everything about him, hesitant to destroy her newfound circumstances should she press for more. But then his naughty notes start to appear, full of humor and wit, and she realizes 'tis likely too late—for her heart may already be his...

Lusty Letters—Ready to savor Daniel's unplanned wooing of his new mistress? Grab your copy today.

A FREE STORY - THE PIRATE'S PLEASURE

Want more steamy, Regency goodness? Sign up for my newsletter, learn of new releases and contests, and as a thanks, I'll send you *The Pirate's Pleasure.*

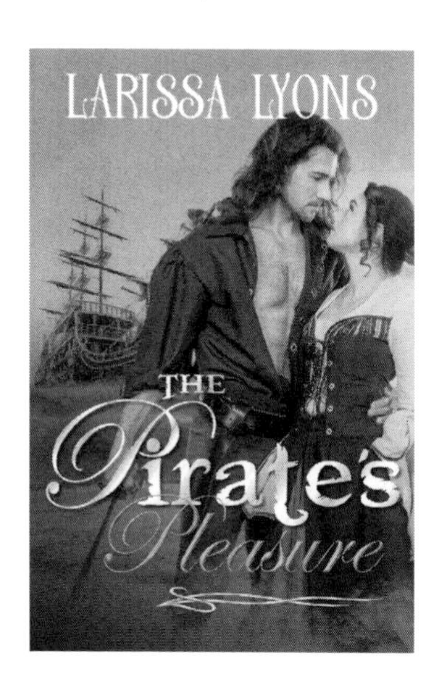

Fresh from rejecting yet another suitor (determined to resist Mama's pressure to accept *anyone*—"Please, dear, before you're so far on the shelf it topples!"), Lady Roberta convenes a weekly writing group comprised of her three closest friends. Their literary efforts soon evolve—or devolve, depending upon one's point of view—from composing insipid lines of poetry to more erotic endeavors.

4000 words • Complete Story • Subscriber exclusive

Meet the ladies and read *The Pirate's Pleasure* here: http://bit.ly/pirates-pleasure

---

If you'd like to sample my contemporary writing in a steamy short, here's *O (Oh! Ohhh!) Christmas Tree.*

I thought we were going Christmas tree shopping with my boyfriend's parents.

He had other ideas.

Sexy, snowy ideas sprinkled with enough sparks to melt any protests I might've made. Making snow angels has never been so naughty.

2500 words • Short 'n' Super Steamy • Happy Ending

Available at: http://bit.ly/o-oh-christmas-tree

ABOUT LARISSA

HUMOR. HEARTFELT EMOTION. & HUNKS.

Larissa writes steamy regencies and sexy contemporaries, blending heartfelt emotion with doses of laugh-out-loud humor. Her heroes are strong men with a weakness for the right woman.

Avoiding housework one word at a time (thanks in part to her super-helpful herd of cats >^..^<), Larissa adores brownies, James Bond, and her husband. She's been a clown, a tax analyst, and a pig castrator (!) but nothing satisfies quite like seeing the entertaining voices in her head come to life on the page.

Writing around some health challenges and computer limitations, it's a while between releases, but stick with her...she's working on the next one.

Learn more at LarissaLyons.com.

facebook.com/AuthorLarissaLyons
instagram.com/larissa_lyons_author
amazon.com/author/larissalyons
bookbub.com/authors/larissa-lyons
goodreads.com/larissalyons

MORE BANG-UP REGENCIES

Ensnared by Innocence
STEAMY REGENCY SHAPESHIFTER

Changing into a lion isn't all fur and games.

A Regency lord battles his inner beast while helping an innocent miss, never dreaming how he'll come to care for the chit—nor how being near his world will deliver danger right to her doorstep.

If Darcy possessed a roaring libido and grappled with feline curses...

Lady Francine Montfort may have led a sheltered life till her parents' untimely demise but that doesn't mean she's ignorant. Neither is she blind to the conniving ways of her persistent aunt, who's determined to marry Francine off for her own selfish gain. Forced to drastic measures to avoid the wretched woman's scheming, Francine concocts her own masterful plan.

She might need to beg a favor from Lord Blakely —the sinfully alluring marquis who inspires all manner of illicit thoughts—but she's determined to help him as well. To ease those mysterious, haunting secrets that torment him so...

When Lady Francine, the epitome of innocence, requests he pose as her betrothed, Blakely knows he should handily refuse. He's baffled when unfamiliar, protective urges make themselves known, tempting him to agree while danger stalks ever closer.

Alas, it's fast approaching the season when Blakely loses all control. Either Francine satisfies his sexual appetites or he'll be forced to reveal his beastly side. And that will never do. Not now that he's come to care for the intrepid miss.

Standalone ~ HEA ~ 80,000-word Novel ~ Book 1 - Roaring Rogues

Regency Shifters

Note: This love story between two people contains some profanity and a lot of sizzle, including one partial ménage scene that gets rather...growly.

Lady Scandal

Sparks—and stockings—fly when an interview for a husband turns into a game of forfeits—played with articles of clothing—a scandalous lady and one handsome rogue learn how very right for each other they are.

Lady Scandal **awarded the Golden Nib!** "I can't praise this book enough. Regency fans, if you like gorgeous wit in with your devilishly superb, well written, sexy reading matter, *Lady Scanda*l should be on your 'Must Read' list." *Natalie, Miz Love & Crew Love's Books*

Top Pick from ARe Café: "[Lady Scandal] is the most flirtatious, sensual, and delectable treat." *Lady Rhyleigh, ARe Café* ~ Selected as a **Recommended Read**!

Mistress in the Making Trilogy

A fun, emotionally satisfying, steamy tale told in three parts: Seductive Silence, Lusty Letters, and Daring Declarations.

Seductive Silence , Part 1

Lord Tremayne has a problem. He stammers like a fool—at least that's what he learned from his father's constant criticism and punishing hand. Daniel now hides his troubles by barley saying anything. But then he goes looking for a new mistress and finds a delightful young woman who makes him, of all people, want to spout poetry. He thought he had a problem before? Avoiding meaningless dinner prattle is nothing compared to the challenge of winning the heart of his new lady lust.

Lusty Letters, Part 2

Thea's fascinating new protector has secrets—several. Hesitant to destroy her newfound circumstances, she stifles her longing to know everything about the powerfully built—and frustratingly quiet—Marquis. But then his naughty notes start to appear, full of humor and wit, and Thea realizes she's about to break the cardinal rule of mistressing—that of falling for her new protector. *Egad.*

Daring Declarations, Part 3

An evening at the opera could prove Lord Tremayne's undoing when he and his lovely new paramour cross paths with his sister and brother-in-law. Introducing one's socially unacceptable strumpet to his stunned family is *never* done. But Daniel does it anyway. And it might just be the best decision he's ever made, for Thea's quickly become much more than a mistress—and it's time he told her so.

Miss Isabella Thaws a Frosty Lord

Blind from a young age, a Regency heroine risks her overbearing father's displeasure by attending a house party, never dreaming she'll meet a formidable lord who will discover all her secrets and still want her for his own.

Top Pick! "This entertaining read conjured up the atmosphere and exquisitely formal dance of manners so beloved in Jane Austen's books...I am enchanted by the grace and artful wordplay that accompanies this tale." *ELF, Night Owl Reviews*

"I love the way that the book reads as if it were written in Regency times. I'm a fan of Carla Kelly Regency romances and I was in the mood for another story of that caliber. I definitely got that with *Miss Isabella Thaws a Frosty Lord*." *EKDuncan*

Historicals by Larissa Lyons

ROARING ROGUES REGENCY SHIFTERS

Ensnared by Innocence (August 2021)

Deceived by Desire (Fall 2021)

Tamed by Temptation (2022)

MISTRESS IN THE MAKING series (Complete)

Seductive Silence

Lusty Letters

Daring Declarations

FUN & SEXY REGENCY ROMANCE

Lady Scandal

A SWEETLY SPICY REGENCY

Miss Isabella Thaws a Frosty Lord

Contemporaries by Larissa Lynx

SEXY CONTEMPORARY ROMANCE

Renegade Kisses

Devastating Kisses (TBA)

Starlight Seduction

SHORT 'N' SUPER STEAMY

A Heart for Adam...& Rick!

Braving Donovan's

No Guts, No 'Gasms

POWER PLAYERS HOCKEY series

*My Two-Stud Stand**

*Her Three Studs**

The Stud Takes a Stand (2022)

*Her Hockey Studs - print version